THE WALLS OF PRIMUS BOOK ONE

OFFENDER

MICHAEL BROOKS

OFFENDER

Cover design by Mikey Brooks/Lost Treasure Illustrating

Published by:
Lost Treasure Publishing & Illustrating, an independent studio.

Summary: In a distant future, all criminals of violent crimes are sentenced to life in the Arena where they must battle against both man and beast in a fight to the death. When sixteen-year-old Calvin Sawyer is wrongly convicted of his father's murder, his charmed life as the son of a senator is changed forever. He's stripped of his rights, his humanity, even his name. Now as the property of the Arena, offender CS4521 must learn to fight in the colosseum. It's kill or be killed.

Hardback Edition

ISBN: 1-939993-84-9
ISBN-13: 978-1-939993-84-7

For Barrett, who showed me what it's like to be strong.

In retribution of acts of violent crimes committed on citizens of Primus, and after a guilty verdict by trial, offenders are to be stripped of their civil rights and liberties, becoming the property of the government of Primus, and thus sentenced to life in the Arena.

—Edict Number Six

OFFENDER

THEY SAY I KILLED MY FATHER, AND NOW I WILL pay the price. I've seen the footage. The proof. They must be right.

The judge's eyes look away from me as he pans the crowd. Dread fills my stomach, as if a vise grips my waist, squeezing tighter and tighter. I say a silent prayer, asking God to forgive the unforgivable.

"I regret this," the judge says, "considering how young you are, but I am bound by the laws of the land. By the authority given me by the senate of Primus, I hereby sentence you, Calvin T. Sawyer, to life in the Arena for the crime of patricide. This sentence shall be carried out immediately."

The gavel slams down, and the room erupts in a roar of voices.

I stand numb, my body frozen but my mind reeling. I don't want to believe what just happened, but the reality of it surrounds me, suffocates me. I try to speak, to tell them they've made a mistake, but I can't—I'm guilty. My life ended with the fall of that gavel. I'd hoped for a lighter sentence: life in the prison mines, exile to the wastelands, anything but the horrors that await me in the Arena.

I'm too young to have my life cut so short.

I won't last five minutes.

"Cal! Cal!"

I hear her voice above the others. I force my head to turn. I have to see her—to memorize her face. The restraints around my wrists tighten, and two guards come toward me. I spin around, searching the crowd for her.

"Mary!" I shout. Flashes from hovercams half blind me. I will my eyes to see past the light. "Mary!"

"Cal!"

I find her. Her honey-blonde hair falls in her face, and her cheeks are wet with tears, but she's still beautiful. She presses against the invisible field that separates me from the crowd. Her parents try to pull her back, but she resists them. I run to her, but the restraints around my wrists yank me back. I pull harder, ignoring the synthetic wire as it cuts into my skin. *I have to tell her the truth. She has to know.*

The guards grab my arms. I fight as they pull me toward a door. *I can't go through it. I can't let this be the end.*

"NO! I have to say goodbye!"

Mary beats her fists on the barrier. "Cal! Cal, I—"

Her words are cut off with the slam of the steel door.

"NO!" I struggle, but the guards are unmoved. The more I fight, the tighter they grip me—the tighter my wrist restraints become. I barely catch sight of another guard before a cloth bag is shoved over my head. I fight again but receive a punch to the gut for my efforts. I try to hunch forward, but the guards hold me up. A thick fist, as solid as an iron hammer, slams into my stomach again. This time my breath, along with my fight, is driven out of me.

"Calm down, Calvin, or the next one won't be so friendly," a voice says. "Get him on the train. If he gives you any problems—inject him."

The guards readjust my weight, dragging me away backwards. My own breath is hot and suffocating against the fabric over my head. The only view I have is a sliver of light shining up from the ground. I want so much more. The restraints slowly loosen on my wrists as I calm down. Warm blood trickles over my hands.

I hear the clank of metal on metal and the purr of a well-oiled motor. A cool breeze blows over my arms, but while I invite the fresh air up my blindfold, it never comes. The muffled sounds of the city surround me. I wish, as I had with Mary, that I could take one last glance at it. To memorize the way it looks, feels, and smells. To remember what it was like to live.

"Is that the kid?" someone calls.

"Yeah," one of my captors replies. "He was putting up a good fight there for a minute, but he gave up."

"They always do, don't they?" The men exchange laughs at my expense. I think about trying to break free of them, just to give them a show, but my wrists and stomach hurt too much. They can have me. I'm dead anyway.

"Stick him in the last car and make sure you double check his restraints. Last week I got a fist to the eye because one of you idiots slacked off."

"I'll check them twice," my guard says. They haul me forward and I hear the swish of a door opening. I'm dragged a few more feet and thrown to the ground. My knees hit the metal floor and searing pain shoots up my legs. I roll over but before I can complain, my ankles are grabbed and the shoes torn from my feet. I feel the cold sting of another restraint locking my ankles together.

Pain rends through me as a steel-toe boot pounds into my stomach over and over. I try to call out but a pop sounds in my chest and my breath catches. The blows continue. They've broken ribs, for sure.

Just when I think I can't take it anymore, the kicking stops. Somewhere between my groans and the urge to throw up, I silently wish to die. Then I laugh inwardly. *Isn't that why I'm here?*

I hear the guards' boots back away, followed by the whoosh of the door again.

I lie in smothering darkness. I want to curl into a ball, to hug my knees to my chest like a child, but the pain screams when I move, so I try to lie as still as I possibly can. The floor shudders, and I feel the motion of the train as it lurches forward. I wonder how long it will take to get there. *Hours or days?* Every mile forward is a mile closer to the Arena … closer to my death.

I pull the cloth sack from my head. I don't bother opening my eyes. I can already tell the car has no windows. I'm still surrounded by darkness but at least now I can breathe.

For what feels like years I sleep, and wake to stare into black nothingness. I think of Mary, of what I should have told her before they found me with my father's bleeding body. Mary deserved the truth. All she wanted was to be loved, and I couldn't even do that right. *Why couldn't I have told her when I had the chance?*

My body rocks forward and I can tell the train is slowing even as my heart begins to pound in my chest. *Will they throw me into the Arena right away?* I'm too weak to fight—it's already enough effort to breathe. Putting me in there now would bring a quick end to my troubles. Then again, I know this is just as much about entertainment as it is about justice. The Arena has to put on a good show. Throwing a beat up sixteen-year-old in a den of lions won't boost ratings. No, they'll want me to suffer. And for as long as possible.

The train stops.

My heart pounds, and rushing blood fills my ears. I breathe heavily as fear pumps through me. Any moment now the door will open and there'll be no escaping the brutal imaginings of those that control the Arena.

The door slides open and daylight burns my eyes. I see

nothing but blurry figures as I'm picked up and placed on a gurney. The restraints at my wrists and ankles are exchanged for steel straps that bite into my skin, binding me to the cold, metal table. The surface beneath my back isn't solid—there are gaps, like grating, and I wonder what they're for.

"Please ... can I have some water?" My voice sounds pathetic and childlike.

"No talking," one of the shadows says.

The table is either hovering or on wheels, because it glides smoothly away from the light and into a dim hallway. I can see better now—two men in crimson uniforms walk in front of me, two behind. The walls seem to be made of glass. I turn my head and see another boy with messy brown hair and blue eyes lying on a table. It takes me a minute before I realize that boy is me.

The men maneuver me into a room with bright, fluorescent lights. Stainless steel tables line the walls, the monitors resting on them flipping through random images of me. There I am, reaching out for Mary in the courtroom. Then standing over my father. There's so much blood my eyes sting at the sight, and the pictures all blur into one red image.

"Who's up this time?" a female voice asks.

A slender woman comes into view. She's probably in her mid-thirties and stands next to a stainless steel table covered with what looks like surgical equipment. She lifts a tablet and taps out a few commands with her middle finger.

"Ah … Thaddeus Sawyer's boy." She says it like she knows me, or at least knew my father. She avoids looking me in the eyes. "Let's start with the scrub."

"Scrub?" I ask.

"No talking," I'm told again.

One of the men grabs a strange looking pair of scissors off the table and places it against my right ankle. Its touch is cold as the man drags it up my calf and over my knee. I hear and feel my clothes being removed as he works his way toward my neck. Goosebumps ripple over my exposed body. I tense and wish I hadn't. The pain in my ribs reminds me to hold still. Another man grabs what's left of my clothing and pulls it away. He tosses it into a glass box, and the fabric spontaneously combusts. A small wisp of smoke is all that is left, then soon, it is gone.

The woman taps in a few more commands on her tablet and two metal restraints cross over me; one over my chest, the other over my waist. The table lifts up so that I'm vertical and my body leans into the restraints. A groan escapes my lips as my ribs rebel against this new position.

"Don't move," the scissor man orders as he raises a pair of shears to my head. I don't move. The shears hum as they run along my scalp and over my crown. Hair falls down my face and onto my chest. It sticks on my lips and I try to blow it away.

The woman glances at me before returning to her tablet. My table, or rack, moves back into an alcove in the room.

White tiles shine around me. A sudden hiss makes me jump, and hot water blasts my skin. It hurts as it runs over my torso and wrists. It sprays in my face and I try not to choke on it but silently thank the moisture that wets my lips and tongue.

"That's enough," the woman says. "Now scrub him down."

The men, who now wear white protective gear covering their faces, come toward me with coarse sponges. They scrub at every inch of me until I feel like they've removed a layer of skin. I do my best not to cry out, but the pain is too great when they attack my ribs.

"You're injured, CS4521," the woman says. "Who injured you? We expect healthy offenders to play in the Arena."

I say nothing. The woman steps forward and her eyes finally connect with mine. Hers are unfeeling and slate-gray. She motions for the men to stop scrubbing, and they back out of the alcove. She gives me a smile. I'm not sure if it's friendly or not.

"Perhaps you didn't realize I was speaking to you," she says, showing no expression. "Let me enlighten you about how things work around here. As an offender in the Arena, you are no longer a citizen of Primus. Do you know what that means?"

I shake my head.

"It means that you have no rights, no allegiance, no name. You are hereby assigned the identification code CS4521. You will answer to this and nothing else. If you are asked your name, you are to give CS4521. Do I make myself clear, CS4521?"

"Yes, ma'am."

"Very well." Her eyes drop back to her tablet and she taps in more commands. Warm air suddenly blasts me from all directions. It heats me until my skin is dry and red. The rack moves me forward and I stop directly in front of the table filled with surgical equipment. I tense and my heart begins to race once more.

The woman suppresses a laugh. "Don't worry, those aren't for you. You're from one of the cities, so you were given a tracking chip the day you were born. We probably could have skipped the scrub. It's really only used for those picked up outside or too close to the borders of Primus. We wouldn't want any radiation contaminating the Arena, now would we? But why skip the scrub when it's so … fun."

Her eyes deliberately glance over my naked body and I cringe. She notices my discomfort and the strange smile returns to her lips. She hovers her tablet over my abdomen and follows the bruises up to my ribs. Her tongue makes a clicking sound and she taps her finger on its screen.

"Now then." Her smile widens. "Are you going to tell me who injured you? How can I expect you to fight well if you're broken?"

"I don't know," I say. "They covered my face."

Her smile vanishes and her eyes narrow. I feel like she's waiting for me to confess some great sin. "Good for them," she says with no expression. "That's smart on their part. Interfering with the Arena is a violation against the senate."

She grabs a large syringe off the table and without so much as a warning, jabs it into my upper thigh. Warmth spreads out from the syringe as she presses down on the plunger.

"What's that?" I ask, my voice stronger than I expected.

"No talking," one of the guards warns. He steps out from the shadows and holds out a baton threateningly.

"Lucky for you," the woman says, ignoring the guards, "we are equipped with the highest advances in nanorobotics. You can expect that rib to be healed just in time for your first fight." Once again her tablet is in hand and she taps in a few more commands. The rack flips forward until I'm facing the burnished steel floor. The restraints tighten as gravity pulls on me. The woman undoes a hinge on the table directly behind my neck and shoulders. I flinch, tensing again.

"This will only hurt for a moment."

Pain stings the back of my neck and I cry out. The searing hot sting continues down my neck and across my shoulders and upper back. Finally the burning stops and I open my eyes. Drool snakes its way from my mouth to the floor. Without warning the restraints open, and I slap painfully to the ground.

"For convenience, your identification code has been branded," the woman says. "Should you forget, have someone tell you."

A stack of gray clothes drops to the floor next to me.

"This is your uniform. You are to wear it at all times except for bathing or fighting. Once you enter the Arena, you will be given a new set of clothes for that. I suggest you dress quickly. We only serve the offenders two meals a day and mealtime is just about over. Welcome to the Arena, CS4521."

-TWO-

FOUR GUARDS, DRESSED IN THE SAME BLOOD-red uniform as the others, and wearing reflective masks, escort me down a long cement corridor. We pass several thick steel doors that have to be unlocked simultaneously with electronic passkeys by two of the guards. Soon we come to an elevator, where once again the guards pull out their passkeys. My mind fills with possible escape routes, considering all the ways I could get out. But then I realize there's really only one true escape: death.

We step into the elevator where I'm forced to stare at the back wall. My stomach lurches as we plummet downward. A steady rhythm of beeps signals each floor as we pass—I stop counting after twenty. By the time the elevator comes to a stop, my legs are tired and I'm trying not to be sick. I want to sleep. Exhaustion clings to me but I suspect sleep won't come any time soon.

One of my guards jabs me in the back. "Move it, CS4521. I don't have all day."

Stiffly, I step out of the elevator. The floor is cold on my bare feet. Beyond the hallway's glass wall I can see a large open area. *Is this the prison? If so, where are all the inmates?* The wall glimmers—forceproof glass. We had the same glass in our windows at home. As a member of the senate, my father feared a possible assassination, so he'd always taken great care to make sure our home was protected. *I wonder if he ever feared me?*

A loud beep sounds as the door at the end of the hall opens. I can see just beyond it is yet another forceproof barrier. I wait for the guards to move but they stand still. I stand with them and get another jab to the back.

"You go in alone," the guard says. "No way in hell I'm going in there."

I shuffle forward a few steps, then look back at the four guards, wishing I could see the faces hidden behind their masks. They stand as still as statues while I'm faced with my reflection where their faces should be. Fear fills me with dread. *What horrors await me behind that glass barrier?* Death, for sure. But at this point, death would be a relief. There are far worse things that could be done to a person before they die.

One guard steps forward and shoves my shoulder. "Move it!"

I turn, face the long hallway, and take a hesitant step.

I get a kick to my backside. I fly forward, fall to my knees, and slide on the glossy floor until I crash against the forceproof wall. I hear a loud beep followed by a hiss. The door behind me locks. I watch my guards return to the elevator. One of them gives another guard a bump with his fist as they pass. I imagine them laughing at my expense. For the first time since my trial, a little courage returns. I ignore the pain in my side and stomach and push up off the floor. I glare at the guards. I don't know if they are looking at me or not, but I try to stand proud. The way my father taught me.

The elevator closes and I'm left staring at the steel door. Another beep sounds, this time behind me.

I turn in time to see the wall behind me sliding open. When I hear the distant rumble of voices, I try not to panic. Try to hold onto my pride. I'll need it if I'm going to survive.

I step into the open area. The floor is polished cement—cold on my bare feet and reflecting everything in sight. Several red, glowing dots stretch across the floor, leading to a dozen or more cameras mounted high on the ceiling. I'm sure down one of the halls that extend to my left and right are the convicts, or what that woman called *the offenders*. I can hear them, but don't see them. How many are there? Do they fight here in this compound, or do they save it for the Arena? *Please, let it only happen in the Arena.*

Pushing myself to be confident, I straighten as best I can with a broken rib, and walk toward the voices. Holding my breath to a count of ten, I push through the door.

It's a cafeteria with hundreds of men crowding the stainless steel tables and benches bolted to the floor. Probably to keep the offenders from using them as weapons.

Everyone wears the same gray shirt and pants as me, no one has shoes, and only a few of them have long hair. The men are eating, laughing with each other or watching the large screens suspended from the ceiling, broadcasting the news. I tense when my face fills the screens. Not me at the trial or even before it. It's me right now. My head is shaved and I'm wearing the gray uniform of an offender.

Instantly the room is silent and every eye falls on me.

"Calvin T. Sawyer, now known as offender CS4521, just entered the Arena's compound," the news anchor announces. "He was convicted yesterday of brutally killing his father, Senator Thaddeus Sawyer, earlier this month."

The screens flick to the footage of me kneeling beside my father's dead body in our home. I'm holding the letter opener in one hand, and I'm covered in my father's blood. I'm still wearing the clothes I had on from the night before. The night I told him I would kill him. I close my eyes and order myself not to show emotion. I cannot let these men know the regret and pain I feel at the loss of my father. They need to see I am strong.

The screen returns to the news desk where a man and woman sit in comfortable chairs. The image of me walking into the cafeteria plays on a screen behind them. The man continues my story. "This young man has actually been causing quite the stir throughout the community, wouldn't you say, Carolyn?"

"Quite right, Mark," she says. "In fact, during the trial,

several riots flared just outside the courthouse. Many are not happy with the conviction of someone so young."

The man nods and goes on. "Calvin … I mean offender CS4521, will be the youngest convict to enter the Arena. The protesters need to remember he was not only tried as an adult, but that the prosecution had exceptional proof of his guilt—including that damning footage of him just after committing his terrible crime. The crime of killing his own father, Senator Sawyer. Still, it is hard to contemplate a teen facing off against some of the more infamous Arena convicts. Hopefully it will be a swift execution instead of a drawn out battle."

"Let's hope you're right, Mark. A swift execution just might appease the protestors. The last thing we need is more violence to come from CS4521's heinous crime."

I am sickened by how freely they talk about my death. As if I'm no longer a human being at all. The news anchors begin talking about my father's replacement in the senate, and I tune them out, my gaze drifting down to find hundreds of pairs of eyes boring into me. *Are they sizing me up? Wondering how a kid like me could be so disturbed as to commit patricide? Or is this how they welcome everyone?*

Someone clears their throat and another man laughs. Soon the men return to their food or conversations. I let out the breath I've been holding. I shuffle toward the end of the food line as it snakes along the back wall. The hairs on the back of my neck prick up, and I turn my head.

There, leaning against the wall to my right, a man stares at me with one intense, dark eye. He wears an eye patch over his left eye, and I can make out three red lines stretching across that side of his face. His good eye connects with mine and he grins wickedly, as if he wants to add me to his dinner. He turns his wrists and his muscles flex, stretching the seams of his gray shirt. My mind tells me to look away, but I keep staring. I recognize him from watching the show. He's an undefeated champion known to the public as Slaughter. I'd seen him crush a man's head between his hands. I'd seen him slit a man's throat and gorge on the blood. Seeing him in person reminds me of the men locked away with me. They are killers. Ruthless and without mercy.

The men around him laugh as they turn to scowl at me. They glance back to Slaughter as if waiting for a signal. I tense, wondering if this moment is where I find my end.

"Keep moving and don't look at them," a man whispers in my ear as he passes. Broken from my trance, I follow after him toward the food along the wall. I focus on his dark brown skin and the tattoo peeking out from his shirt. He is HW11. I figure he's been in the Arena for a while. Not just because his ID is much shorter than mine, but because his dark, graying hair is long and tied up in a knot. I also vaguely remember him fighting on the show. He's big, almost as big as Slaughter. HW11 tosses his disposable plate into a bin and grabs another off a stack next to the counter of food. I reach out for a plate and steal a glance back at Slaughter. He and his fellow inmates are still watching me intently. I cringe and turn away.

"You're not too bright, are you?" HW11 whispers. He grabs a chicken leg from the counter of food and tosses it on his plate. "You don't want to get their attention. You best keep as far away from them as you can." He grabs an apple and stashes it in his pants pocket.

"Thanks, HW11," I whisper back.

HW11 drops his plate on the counter and grabs me by my shirt. My rib screams in pain as he pulls me so close our noses touch.

"That. Is. Not. My. Name."

He pushes me and walks away, not forgetting to grab his plate. I step back and wipe the spit from my face. As he leaves, I double check his tattoo. I can clearly see HW11 branded there. I watch him until he leaves the cafeteria, then glance around at the others seated at the tables. No one seemed to notice. They continue to eat and talk. Even Slaughter and his cronies have found something else to focus on.

I grab a plate from the stack just as a bell rings. I reach for a chicken leg but before I can grab one, the food sinks into the counter and a steel cover shields it. A few of the men laugh at me as they deposit their empty plates in the bin next to me.

"Hey, stiff," one of them says. "Hope you like being hungry."

"Hope you like being dead," another jeers.

They laugh and join the line of offenders out of the cafeteria. I scan the crowd of men, trying to see if I recognize any of the Arena champions from the show. I think better of it when I spot Slaughter and his men coming toward me. Quickly, I step in line with the other offenders and try my best to get out of the cafeteria without bringing any more attention to myself. The men head out of the hall into the open area, and I follow. Some wave up at the ceiling cameras as if saying hi to a friend. I wonder if I waved, would Mary see it? I go to lift my hand but decide not to. I hope she never sees me like this.

Someone shoves me hard in the chest. My rib blossoms with pain, but I glare into the face of the man who pushed me. He has a serpent-dragon tattoo over his jawline. He looks vaguely familiar, probably from watching the show.

"Where'd you think you're goin'?" he hisses. "Ones don't belong here."

I shake my head. "I … I don't know what you're talking about."

"Buzz off, stiff, this hall's for fives."

Another offender behind him snickers. "Go easy on him, Dragon. The kid's new."

"You tellin' me what to do?"

"Yeah, I am," the guy says, getting in Dragon's face. "You wanna make something of it? Because I'll make something of it, real fast."

Dragon rolls his eyes and pushes him away. "You need to lay off the onions before you go blowin' in my face."

They laugh and Dragon turns back to me. "You got an ID, right, kid?"

I nod.

"The last digit is your assigned group." He points toward the elevator. "Ones go down the first hall."

"What do the other numbers mean?" I ask.

"What's this? Do I look like a shankin' school teacher? Buzz off, kid, before I take your head off." Dragon shoves me in the shoulder, then he and his friend continue down their assigned hall.

I step into the line Dragon indicated, and follow it toward the other side of the open area. I check the number on the back of the offender's neck in front of me. His tattoo ends with a one.

"Hey, is this where our rooms are?" I ask. He shoots me a look that would melt metal. I try again. "Look, I don't know where to go. Can you please help me out?"

"Do I look like your nanny, kid?"

I deliberately look him up and down, taking in his bulking frame. "No," I say. "Your breasts are much bigger."

He stops dead in his tracks and the offender behind me stumbles against my back, pushing me forward. "Watch it, stiff."

"Keep your girlfriend in line," the man behind me says as he shoves past us without an apology.

I'm met once again with that metal-melting glare. I put my hands up in surrender. "Look, I'm sorry. Can you just help me, please?"

He continues to glare at me, but his scowl isn't as hard as it was before. I wait, hoping he'll forget the snide remark about his weight. He lets out a long sigh. "Fine," he says. "Follow me."

We head down the glass hallway and past several cells with two bunk beds in each. There's a sink and a toilet in the center of each cubicle and nothing else. I shudder at the thought of no privacy. I guess that was a right that disappeared with my name.

"Hey, thanks," I say.

"Don't mention it. Like … ever. I need to look tough."

"You do."

He laughs. "Yeah, sure. That's why, when some kid gets thrown in here, I'm the first one he comes to for help. It's the round face, right? It's too childlike."

"I actually just saw that you had a one in your ID."

"Whatever," he grunts. "Call me Slim. Everyone else does."

"I was told to only call offenders by—"

"Ignore the shaft you were told. We make our own rules down here. Call me Slim."

"Okay, Slim. I'm Cal."

"No, no," he says with a snort. "It doesn't work that way. You got to be given your name." He pauses for a second as he sizes me up and down. "Considering what everyone is already calling you, it's either Kid or Stiff."

"Stiff?"

"As in dead…you know, a stiff."

"I think I'll take Kid. I'm not dead yet."

"There you go, Kid." We continue down the hallway. "This is you." I've lost count of the cells, there are so many. Slim lets loose a quiet chuckle but barely pauses in front of the cell he's just indicated. "Mom would be proud for me for looking out for you, anyway."

"Huh?" I ask, jogging forward three steps to catch up to him. "What do you mean?"

Slim stops and motions for me to come closer. "Kid, we've been watching your trial all month. We know what an innocent guy looks like. You don't have the same look in your eye as some of these heathens."

"Same look?"

"Don't worry; you'll know it when you see it. Half the guys in here have that look. You can tell which ones enjoy the kill."

His words buzz through my brain and I can't latch onto any of them.

"Boy, did someone screw you over good." He looks up, and I notice there's a camera a few yards away. His voice gets so quiet I can barely hear it. "You ever wonder who did it?"

"Did what?" I whisper.

"Killed your daddy."

I step back, confused at what he's trying to say. *I* killed my father.

Slim lets out a quiet laugh again. "You don't really think you killed him, do you? A kid like you? You must be shankin' nuts in the head. That footage they had of you should have been enough. Didn't you ever wonder why they didn't just throw you in here without a trial—a *real* trial anyway?"

He slaps me on the shoulder and walks away. I stand there for a moment, trying to make sense of his words.

"Hey, Kid," he calls back. I look up and see he's at the end of the hall. "We don't want to be late. The late guys get their skulls cracked."

-THREE-

I SIT NEXT TO SLIM ON THE TOP ROW OF THE metal bleachers that span the right side of the room. In the center of the room is a large, blue mat with white rings on it. I assume it's for some type of training, like martial arts or wrestling. Behind the mat, along the wall, are countless numbers of exercise equipment—rows of bulky treadmills stand beside gray weights with chrome bars. *No wonder these guys all have biceps the size of my waist.*

In the far corner of the room, a doorway leads into an even larger area that looks like a miniature version of the Arena. I recognize some of the structures they've used during man-to-man combats. It's funny now that I think about it. When I was little, I'd pretend I was one of the fighters I'd seen on the screen. Now I wouldn't wish this on my worst enemy.

The last of the men take their place on the bleachers and I wait in anticipation for what will come next. The lights in the room dim, and a screen lowers from the ceiling.

"Time to pick tonight's kitty food," Slim whispers in my ear.

The screen flickers to life with the Arena's familiar logo—the colosseum surrounded by a steel circle that rotates in fire. Under the word Arena is the slogan: *Fight to the Death.* Triumphant music fills the silence. Now I understand what Slim means. This is the Choosing. I watched these as a kid, anxiously waiting for my favorite fighters to be called to battle. Now when I glance around the room, I see some of the men have their heads lowered as if in prayer, others sit up straight and proud as if wanting their numbers called.

"How do they choose the fighters?" I whisper to Slim.

He shakes his head. "No one's been able to figure out the system. It's random. You don't have to worry though—stiffs never get chosen their first week. They want you to train first—attempt to put on a good show, ya know?"

Knowing I'm safe—for the moment—fills me with relief.

"Welcome, everyone, to the Arena!" a feminine voice calls over the music. The logo fades away and the image of the Arena's host fills the screen. Tonight, Scarlet Wild is wearing a white fur robe that trails out behind her beautiful body. Her hair is white with the slightest tint of blue at the tips. It complements the blues in her thick makeup. The CGI background is an arctic landscape. "Tonight you are in for a treat, ladies and gentlemen. Not only will there be a *Fight to the Death* between two of our most ruthless inmates, but I am told a special *Beast Battle* will also take place. Something the likes of which you've never seen."

"This is new," Slim says.

The man to my left has abandoned his prayer and now glares at the screen, his hands clenched together so tightly his knuckles are white. I glance at his eyes and the fear I see there startles me. *Should I be afraid too?*

Scarlet lets out an exaggerated sigh, flirting with the camera. Her fur robe teasingly reveals a frosty blue bikini atop twinkling diamond-studded skin. Some of the men in the room let out whoops of excitement. Scarlet giggles and tries to act embarrassed as if she can hear them. She isn't a very good actress, but she's much better looking than the Arena's last host, who I heard was forced into an early retirement. Scarlet is the new eye candy of nightly entertainment.

"It's so cold tonight," Scarlet goes on. "Maybe I should cover up a bit?"

"NO!" The men behind me yell at the screen. Scarlet giggles again and pulls her fur robe tight around her. The men boo disappointedly. She gives the camera a wink, and the fur robe falls to the ground. The men cheer and Scarlet stands proud and exposed.

"She's so hot, the snow will start melting soon," Slim says.

I roll my eyes. Scarlet Wild may be practically naked, but her beauty's nothing compared to Mary's. Scarlet is fake where Mary is real. An ache forms in the pit of my stomach as I remember the last night we were together. I wish I could have stayed in that moment forever. My arms entwined around her warm body, the smell of her sunshine hair filling my lungs. Oh, how I miss her.

Scarlet continues to blather on, recapping last night's fight, but I'm tuned out, thinking only of my Mary. Is she thinking about me now? Does she know how much I miss her?

"Let's not waste another moment. It's time to select tonight's fighters!" Scarlet's words rip me from my thoughts and my focus returns to the large screen. She extracts a thick scroll from a nearby snowdrift. Slowly, she unrolls it and holds it next to her firm, sparkling stomach. The camera zooms in. Images of the inmates' faces spin across the surface of the scroll. A red square lights up, flicking over the faces as they spin. The spinning stops, the red square highlighting the first combatant. A second red square appears as the images flash again. When the second fighter is selected, Scarlet squeals and bounces up and down. I stretch my neck, trying to catch a glimpse of the faces highlighted on the scroll.

"Our first warrior in tonight's *Fight to the Death*—offender DC66." Slaughter's face, framed in red, fills the screen. "And his challenger—offender WP585." Dragon's face flashes before me. The men in the room let out an audible sigh of relief. As I stare at the screen, I wonder what Dragon must be feeling right now. Sure he's big and pretty intimidating, but obviously he's seen what Slaughter can do. I hope he beats Slaughter, but I know deep down he won't. Dragon is as good as dead.

"Now for our *Beast Battle*," Scarlet says. She closes the scroll and reopens it. Again, images of the inmates' faces speed by. A red square lights up in the center of the screen. The room is as silent as a grave as we all wait to see who of us will be chosen.

The spinning stops.

My body seizes.

It's my face that's highlighted by the red square.

Slim was wrong—I will be fighting tonight.

I hear men's voices, feel hands pounding my back, but I can't make sense of the words. I stare, fixated, at the screen. Scarlet says my identification number and giggles. My picture vanishes from the scroll as she rolls it back up and the camera pans Scarlet's mostly naked body. She tries to giggle again but the shock is prevalent in her eyes. She looks around as if waiting on a cue from someone before returning her focus to the screen.

"There you have our fighters for this evening." She gives a smile that appears forced compared to the bubbly woman that she was just seconds ago. "It looks to me like a night of perfect entertainment. Don't go anywhere. We'll be right back after these select messages from tonight's sponsors." The screen returns to the logo of the Arena, but I can't tear my gaze away. The circle of fire around the colosseum has become blue, spurting tiny snowflakes.

I knew my time in the Arena would be short. I knew I could never fight like these men did. Slim's words gave me hope that I'd at least have time to train, to grow stronger, more able to fight. That's gone now. How can I fight a beast with a broken rib?

"Kid, I'm sorry," Slim says. I hear him, but I don't acknowledge him. I just stare, wishing I'd done things differently. Wishing I'd never fought with my father. That he could've seen things the way I did, to let me love the way I wanted to—to love who I wanted to.

"You have fifteen minutes to suit up," a voice booms. "Come with me." I tear my eyes away from the screen and they fall on the hulking frame of HW11. He's standing in the center of the blue mat, glaring up at me; his brown arms tightly folded around his chest. I wonder briefly if he's still mad for me calling him by his identification number. The rest of the men surround him, some watching me, others staring at the floor. *Is this how they bid farewell to those heading off to die?*

"It's really too bad." Slim reaches out a hand to help me up. I ignore it as I stand up and brush past him on my way to the steps. "Hey," Slim says, grabbing my arm. "I've had a couple of beast battles in my time. The trick is to go for their weak spots."

"Thanks." It doesn't matter. I don't stand a chance.

"Kid, you can win if you believe you can."

I half laugh, half sigh. "That's just it. I don't believe."

I shrug off Slim's hold on my arm and head down the bleacher steps toward HW11. Without a word he motions for me to follow and pushes through the crowd of offenders. The men slap my shoulders as I pass. Each slap is an aching reminder of the beating I got yesterday. Some men mumble words of encouragement while others joke about how I'll barely be a snack for the great beast they'll set against me. A few men try to give me tips like Slim. I don't acknowledge them. No amount of advice will help me now.

HW11 leads me through the practice room and down a hallway. Several cameras line the walls and I wonder if people around Primus are watching me right now. What would Mary think, seeing me sulking like this? Wouldn't she want me to try my best, try to stay alive as long as I can? I straighten. For her, I try to act brave.

We stop at a door, and HW11 punches a series of codes into a keypad affixed to the wall. I want to ask him how he knows the codes, but I don't. I can tell he doesn't like me at all, because I followed the rules. I shouldn't have gotten on his bad side. I guess in a few minutes it won't matter anymore.

The door slides open to a room filled with weapons and armor. I follow HW11 inside and marvel at all the different ways to kill. I reach for a long sword and a shock sends my hand back.

HW11 laughs. "Like I said before, you're not too bright. What? Do you think they just let a bunch of crazy killers have access to all these weapons? Kid, you are messed in the head if you think that."

"Then what are they for?"

"You can choose up to five items, but only two weapons. Choose fast—I don't have all night to babysit your sorry case."

"I don't know what I'm up against."

HW11 shakes his head. "Damn, Kid, no one knows what they're up against. Welcome to the world of the Arena."

"What would you choose?"

He looks me up and down. He laughs. "You couldn't even lift the things I'd choose."

"If you're not going to help, why are you here?"

"Kid, I'm not here to help you. I'm here to punch in the damn code. Now pick your shankin' weapons so I can get on with doing something worth my time."

I ignore him and inspect a wall of weapons. HW11 is right. While I can see a large battle-axe as an effective tool against an animal, the fact is I'm too small to wield it with any kind of effectiveness. I need something light weight, like a gun. I've seen a few fights where the inmates used guns but they were always in group combat. I wonder where they got the guns from. My eyes fall on a collection of staffs toward the back of the room. Each one has a gold plate with a name and date inscribed on it. I read them, thinking of a world lost to history.

Ankus-c.1890, Bardiche-c.1590, German Halberd-c.1480, Polex-c.1470. I estimate their weight and decide on the German Halberd. I like its angled ax blade and long spiked end. The pole might also help keep the animal back.

"I want that one," I say, pointing to the halberd.

"What else," HW11 says. He gives no indication whether he approves of my choice, only pulls a tablet from the bag hanging by his waist and taps in a few keys.

I need both hands to use the halberd so I find a short dagger and point to it. "The quillon dagger."

"You've got three more items and about two minutes left to select them before you forfeit your items."

"What? Never mind!" I try to think back to other beast fights I've seen but I can't recall any. I'm sure I'd seen them. I can remember Mom going on about how brutal they were and how it wasn't appropriate for someone so young to be watching it. I point to a large shield and HW11 laughs. I shake my head. He isn't helping. I try to think back, hoping for clues Scarlet might have given during the choosing. Dad had always said that if you were observant, you can predict the upcoming battle. Good for gamblers, he said. I see a fur cape and remember that for a brief time Scarlet wore fur. I think back to the last image I saw of the Arena's logo; blue fire with snowflakes. Most likely it will be cold. "I want the fur cape and that breast shield."

"Thirty seconds."

A helmet—I see a helmet. "That!"

HW11 taps a bunch of codes into the tablet and a mechanical sound pulls my attention back to the array of weapons. A suspended bar with a robotic arm attached collects my items and whisks them out of sight. A moment later a door next to HW11 slides open.

"You'll find everything through there. You'll only get so much time, so dress fast. Once you're done, press the call button. That'll open the door to the conveyer. It will take you inside the colosseum."

I say nothing as I step through the door.

"If you believe in God, pray now," HW11 says as the door closes behind me.

Three of the walls in the small room are mirrored. One wall is plain, with a glowing white button at chest height. A small, black bench sits in the center of the room. Next to it is a dress form draped in the fur cape I'd chosen, the breast shield, and a leather loincloth. The staff is propped against it and the dagger rests on the floor next to a pair of primitive boots with leather straps.

This moment is so surreal. Like some bad dream I wish I could wake from. But no amount of wishing has saved me yet. I found the letter opener in my blood-covered hands and, since then, the nightmare hasn't stopped and nothing has offered me a way out. Wishes don't come true.

Not wanting to waste any more time, I undress and toss my gray uniform to the corner of the room. I pull the loincloth from the dress form and wrap it around my waist. I've never even imagined myself wearing something like this and it takes me a minute to figure out how it goes on. It takes me even longer to figure out the boots. I do my best and hope they stay on. I grab the dagger and tuck it into my right boot. The breast shield is too big and the way it hangs cuts into my side, assaulting my broken rib. Disappointed, I leave it on the bench. I grab the helmet and pull it on. Like the breast shield, it's too big and muffles the sounds in the room. I pull it off and leave it next to the shield on the floor. Two of my items wasted, I tug the fur cape from the dress form and wrap it around my shoulders, tying the knot under my chin.

When I see my reflection in the mirrors I feel stupid. Any other guy in this prison would look so much better than me in this getup. I'm no warrior. I look like a child—bruised and broken, weak, embarrassed. I'm a child playing dress up, in clothes too big for him.

This is what you deserve, I tell myself. And I know it's true. I killed my father, they say. And I have no proof that I didn't.

One of the mirrored walls flickers, lighting up with the logo of the Arena. It quickly dissolves into the background as a scene of two men standing atop an icy cliff fills the wall. I don't want to watch this. Why do I have to see this before I go in to face my own doom? I turn my eyes away only to find the scene playing all around the room. I sit on the bench and shut my eyes, but suddenly I am encased in a cacophony of sound. I cover my ears, but the roar of the battle only increases, getting louder and louder. They are forcing me to listen to the clanks of metal on metal, the pants of breath, the awful sound of flesh being torn open.

Make it stop, make it stop. But it only gets louder.

Dragon screams and Slaughter laughs, his sickening, childlike squeal fills my ears. More grotesque sounds fill the room, and I grab for the helmet and hold it under my chin, feeling the urge to throw up. My eyes betray me, and I see a room filled with images of blood and carnage. Then as suddenly as it came, the mirrors fade to a skinny sick boy lying on the floor. I'm not sure when I fell off the bench. The glowing white button flashes once, twice, and then deepens to a blood red, reminding me of what I need to do next.

I don't want to, but I press the button. One of the mirrored walls opens, revealing the conveyer. My hands shake, but I tighten my grip on the staff and grit my teeth. I need to look brave for Mary. It's the last thing I can do for her.

I step onto the conveyer and it pulls me into darkness.

THE CONVEYER ENDS AT A SMALL CEMENT room that is empty, except for a small platform along the back wall. A glaring red arrow painted on the cement wall points up, showing me that the platform is a lift that will take me into the Arena. Hesitantly, I step on.

My body shakes as if the platform is unstable—but it's not the lift that's causing tremors to course over my body, it's fear. I close my eyes, clenching my fists at my sides, and force myself to take a deep breath. Then another. I need to be brave. Mary will be watching.

A hiss sounds from the hydraulic pump under the platform, and it lifts me into the air. I pass into a cement tube lined with dim lights that flash past me one by one. Vertigo makes me dizzy, so I squeeze my eyes shut once more. I don't want to be disoriented when I reach the top. Wind rushes around me as the platform lifts me higher and higher. I hear the hiss again and my stomach lurches as the platform comes to a stop. Brightness hits my face and I blink my eyes open.

I am in an arctic wasteland. I see nothing but cliffs of ice and snow all around me. I put out my hand and feel a cold, glass barrier protecting me from that world. I don't see the beast that I have to face, but I know it's out there, waiting. I know it will be monstrous, because that's the way they genetically create them. To be monstrous killers.

Goose bumps ripple up and down my exposed arms and legs as the wall of glass lowers. I can hear the distant roar of people. I know somewhere beyond the digital backdrop before me, the colosseum is filled with thousands of spectators. Every drop of sweat I shed will be seen by the world. Every drop of blood. My heart pounds.

The cold air blankets me in its icy clutches. I can't help the shaking now. I want to pull the fur cape around me, but I know I can't stay here forever. There is nothing to shield me from an attack. The wintry scene before me is barren of trees or any vegetation. Large, dark rocks hide under the shadow of an endless white field of snow. The ground juts up every few hundred feet or so, towering high like the backbone of some great beast. A taller cliff face of rock seems like the best protection. I can use the wall as a line of defense.

I force myself to move. The snow is deep and I fall into it as I step from the platform. It is so cold, it makes my muscles rebel, freezing me in place.

Cal, you have to move, I tell myself. *You have to fight, and you have to win. Don't let Mary see you die this way.*

Obediently, I climb from the snow and race toward a cliff of ice and stone. My eyes scan the ground, searching for tracks, but I don't see any. I try to think back to my lessons from school about the arctic. What animals did they have before the atomic wars? I can picture in my mind short, fat, black and white bird-like things but I can't imagine them being deadly. The Arena would only use lethal animals.

I press my back against the cliff's face and fall through the stone like it's a paper wall. My elbows smack down on a rock floor. Pain shoots up into my shoulders and I cry out. *That was stupid.* I should know better than to trust the landscape. I reach down to massage my elbows and find them covered in sticky blood—not my blood.

Instantly the pungent smell of death fills my nostrils. Immediately my heart is on edge, pounding so rapidly its thud-thud fills my ears.

Scrambling to my feet, I take in my surroundings. It's a cave. A cave covered with the remains of some kind of animal. I see fur and tissue, blood and gore. The burned, bitter smell of decay is too much, and my stomach betrays me. I turn away to retch in a corner, but I have nothing in me, so the dry heaves wrack my body, leaving me feeling shaky and weak. I take a step back, but stumble and fall, landing on the remains of a small cub. Its lower half is missing, but I can tell it's some breed of large cat. Its mouth hangs open in a frozen cry, displaying elongated razor-sharp canine teeth. I recall what this beast is, a saber-tooth. *I have to get out of here.*

Panicking, I crawl out of the cave, dragging my staff with me. The snow is numbing my fingers and knees, but I have to get away. The mother of those cubs will smell the blood. She'll find her cubs, and her rage and bloodlust will make her even more ferocious. I don't stand a chance.

Images of my father's body flash through my mind. His red-stained face. The same horrified expression as the cub in the cave. I collapse to the ground. Again I dry heave. I grab at the snow and scrub the blood from my hands and arms—his blood.

Cheers fill the colosseum. It rips me from my stupor, and I pull myself to my feet. I know what this means. I am no longer alone in this wasteland of ice and snow. I scan the field of white, searching for the mother of the cubs. She is nowhere in sight, but I can't wait for her to come find me. I go to move but the fur cape drags behind me leaving a trail of red in the white snow. I reach up and undo the clasp of the cape. It falls to the icy ground, and I run. I run as I have never run before. I have to get as far away from that cave as I possibly can. The snow pulls on my boots. I fall and try to crawl-swim my way to the top.

A bone-chilling howl fills the air. I can hear the pain in that cry. It's the same pain I felt when I woke to see my father's lifeless eyes. I know I shouldn't, but I look behind me. A large white tail with black stripes swings back and forth. She hasn't started hunting for me yet. But she will. I know she will. I run harder.

I see a mound of rocks and I aim for it, falling twice before I reach it. I scramble over the mound—the rocks are sharp and cut into my knees and the palms of my hands. I ignore the sting and climb higher. Reaching the top of an icy boulder, I spin around toward the cave but I can't see it anymore. I make out my trail of prints—my prints and …

The saber-tooth attacks.

Her roar makes me slip. I go down slapping my stomach against the sharp, icy rock. It cuts into my chest at the same time her giant cat claws slice across my back. I roll over and she loses her balance. She crashes against the stone mound and rolls down the side. I push myself to my feet, trying my best to regain my footing on the mound, ignoring the searing pain in my back and chest. My staff in hand, I stand my ground atop the boulder. The saber-tooth gets to her feet about a third of the way down the rocky mound and shakes the rock dust and snow from her striped fur. She looks up at me and blasts me with a death cry. I wish I could tell her that it wasn't me. That I didn't kill her cubs, but there is no mercy in those golden eyes.

She climbs up the mound with ease, never once taking her eyes off me. I hold my staff out. Its pointed axe blade shines in the sunlight. Slim's advice runs through my mind and I try to calculate the saber-tooth's weak spots. Slim's an idiot. This cat doesn't have any. She lets out a low rumble as she circles me, her eyes never leaving the blade. I can tell she's familiar with weapons. I notice then that her face is scarred with the memories of past battles. I don't want to kill her. I don't think I could live with myself if I did. She's like me, a prisoner to the Arena.

She darts toward me so suddenly that I'm thrown off guard. I turn the staff just in time, and it nicks her muzzle. She attacks again. Claws ready to kill. I step backward and thrust my staff forward. She leaps back with a hiss. I jab my staff toward her once more, forcing her further down the mound. I know she won't back down. This is a fight to the death. It's either me or her.

Again she attacks. I thrust out my staff but it's too low. She leaps. Her mouth stretches wide. I dive toward the ground, but too late. Teeth sink into my shoulder. Pain—horrible, unbearable pain fills me. I steel myself against the agony, fighting desperately not to black out. I have to fight. To win. I beat at her face with my fist and make contact with her eye. She lets go and pulls away for a split second. I grab the staff and hold it across my chest, like a barrier. She clamps her jaw around the wood and chomps the staff in two. She crouches low and growls. I'm as good as dead to her.

With all the energy I have, I drag myself away, the ice helping me to slip further toward the edge of the mound. She doesn't move, only tracks me with her eyes. She knows she has me. I'm nothing more than a mouse to pounce on. The pain in my left arm is gone; it drags beside me, numb and useless, as I back further away. She crouches low, moving her shoulders up and down as if ready for her grand finale.

I reach down and pull the knife from my boot, gripping it in my right hand. It's nothing compared to her magnificence. Not even as long as one of her fangs. Still, I hold it out with one shaking arm as if it's some talisman that will hold her back. She hisses at the weapon and I can see rage in her eye. I push back once more just as she lifts her front legs to leap.

The stone beneath us shifts, she loses her footing, and stumbles into me. The rock mound gives way and we fall. Stone and fur collide with my body as we roll with the tumbling rocks. A burst of pain fills my skull as a rock hits the side of my head. Her wet fur brushes once more against my chest and legs as we crash against more rock. My side hits the stone mound and another rib pops. I roll and fall again. My right leg snaps as I crash down. At the bottom of the mound, I finally roll to a stop.

I don't feel pain anymore. Snowflakes drift lazily down onto the saber-tooth who lies just feet from me. My knife found its way into her throat. She heaves. Blood spurts out as she breathes in. The snow is red. Her beautiful lined fur is stained with spots of blood.

We look at each other and I wonder what she's thinking. What had she done to deserve a life sentence in the Arena? Does she know regret the way I do? Probably not.

I hate myself for hurting something so majestic. She didn't deserve this. Her cubs didn't deserve this. I wish I could tell her that it wasn't me; that I would never hurt her that way. She is innocent—the one thing I wish I was. She gives one last moan and her eye closes. Her breathing stops but the snow continues to fall. Beautiful, really.

I lie there for what feels like eternity. Perhaps I will be buried alongside the saber-tooth in a frozen grave of snow and ice. I can feel my life slipping away. I can't move, but I don't want to anyway. This death is peaceful. It's so silent and still with the fall of the snow that I don't want to leave it.

"Mary," I say. "I'm sorry."

I close my eyes and let oblivion take me.

-FIVE-

MARY'S BODY IS WARM, AND THE SMELL OF her honey-gold hair reminds me of sunshine. She breathes in slow and deep. Somewhere between homework and kissing, she fell asleep. My arm begins to tingle under her neck, but I try not to move. I don't want to interrupt her slumber. She's perfect this way—*we* are perfect this way.

I set down my homework tablet. Reading up on an almost forgotten battle fought in 1570 between the Spanish and the Turks doesn't seem as interesting as holding her. I spoon in next to her back, wrapping my free arm around her waist. She moves, nestling in closer. I ache to kiss her again.

"I love you, Cal."

She says it so quietly I wonder if she's dreaming.

I'm not sure how to respond, or even if I should. I've never told anyone that I loved them. I don't even recall ever hearing it myself. Perhaps my mother told me, but it must've happened so long ago that I've forgotten. My father doesn't use words like love. He's not affectionate in that way. He's a leader—and leaders lead with their minds, not their hearts.

Mary moves again, and now I feel her stroking my forearm with her fingers. I know she's waiting—wanting me to say it. I open my mouth but nothing comes out. *Why can't I say it?* I've said things I didn't really mean before. I can lie. But I don't want to, not to her.

"Is it too soon?" she asks.

Maybe. Then again, probably not. We'd been seeing each other for months, since the beginning of school when we found each other under the apple tree in the schoolyard. Even then I knew there was something different about her. It wasn't just her looks, because everyone could see how beautiful she is—the difference was deeper. She was kind in ways I didn't understand. She'd been under the apple tree helping a bird that had been knocked from its nest. She had compassion for life. Something I didn't see a lot of in my house.

"I should probably get going before your dad gets home." She shifts, but I hold her tight against me.

"I don't want you to leave. I like this. I like you and me."

"I like this too, Cal, but it's getting late and I don't want my parents to get the wrong idea."

"What? We did our homework."

"We did more than that."

"Hardly," I tease. "A kiss or two, maybe."

She rolls over and presses her lips into mine. They are soft and her lip balm smells like strawberries. I move my hands to her neck and down her shoulders. She pulls away and smiles. "There. Now you've had a little more." The ache of wanting her returns. I try to kiss her again but she pulls away. "Cal, we can't."

A knock sounds on my bedroom door, and before I can even answer, it opens. Dad's eyes dart from me to Mary. Instantly I feel embarrassed. Not because he caught me lying on my bed with a girl, but because of the smug expression on his face. As if he's pleased I've finally taken an interest in something other than reading books on my tablet, and it's a girl.

"Hi, Dad," I say, getting up. "We were just going over some homework. We have a history test tomorrow."

"Homework," he repeats as he watches Mary get off my bed and reach down to pick up her jacket and bag. I feel irritation as he continues to stare after her every movement.

I step in front of Mary. "Did you need something?"

Broken from his spell, he gives me a smile. "I have a few members of the senate here for dinner. They wanted to meet you."

"They want to meet me? Since when do they care about me?"

"Probably since you were announced top in your class this afternoon." He's smiling now. I'm dumbfounded.

"Me? But I—"

"That's great, Cal," Mary says, coming to my side. "That must make you very proud, Senator Sawyer."

"Yes, it does," he says. "Calvin is making strides in his education. Something I expect out of the future consul of Primus."

"Consul?" I ask. "Dad, you know I'm not interested in the politics of—"

"I don't believe we've properly met." He holds out his hand to Mary. She takes it.

"I'm Mary Omphrey. I go to school with Cal."

He smiles at her as he would any registered voter. "Omphrey, is it? I don't recall ever hearing that name. Your parents obviously aren't in government. What's their profession?"

She hesitates, and I know why. Her parents work at the school as groundskeepers. If he learns that, he'll know what they are. I try to change the subject.

"That's great about my ranking. Do you know who came in second? Or even third? I'd like to know who my competitors are."

He ignores me completely. "Where do your parents work?"

Mary goes to say something but he pulls forward on her hand and yanks up her sleeve. His face angers at the sight of the blue mark on her arm. The one declaring her a defector—those who chose to abandon Primus during the atomic wars but returned because of sickness or starvation. He throws her hand back at her and his angry, steel-blue eyes fix on me. "You brought one of them into my house? How dare you?"

"She's done nothing wrong," I shout. "Look at her imprint, she's fifth generation. Not even her parents can be—"

"I don't care how many generations it goes back. They are traitors to the Lands of Primus. I have five members of the senate downstairs. How do you think they will react to my son harboring filth like this?"

"She's not filth!"

"Get out of my house!" he orders her. "You will no longer associate yourself with my son. He is done with you. We do not accept what you are. Your kind will never—"

"You can't tell me who I can and can't associate with," I scream. "Mary's my girlfriend."

"Not anymore." He steps away from the door and points down the hall. "Get out of my house, defector."

Mary's lips quiver, and tears are in her eyes. She grabs her backpack and runs past me.

"Mary!" She flies down the steps and I follow after her. "Mary, wait."

"Calvin," Dad warns. I ignore him, but he grabs hold of my arm.

I pull away but he takes a fierce hold. "Let me go."

Again I try to pull away, but suddenly my right eye and cheek explode with pain. I cup my face and crumple to the floor. I look up and see rage in Dad's eyes. He is so angry spit flies at me as he shouts.

"How dare you bring that into my house? How dare you? I did not raise you to be so stupid, so naïve. You know the implications of that filth coming in here. Your mother would be mortified to see this. You've shamed her name!"

I know it's not true. Mom would've loved Mary regardless of the blue brand on her arm. They were alike, both kind—not like him.

"I hate you," I whisper. He doesn't hear it.

"Get up and act like a man," he orders. "I have important people downstairs and now I have to come up with an explanation for your foolishness."

"Why? I'm not the one who threw her out. I'm not the one who didn't even bother to see that she's done nothing. It's not her fault the law—"

He slaps me again, this time catching my lip. "I AM THE LAW!"

"I hate you," I say as I stand. "I hate you and your stupid laws. I hate you and I wish you were dead!"

"Is everything all right?" Margret, our housekeeper, asks. The stunned expression on her face says she's seen him strike me. Dad waves her away with his hand, but she holds her ground, waiting, as if reminding him that people are watching.

I rub my cheek. I can barely open my right eye, but I stand tall and proud, the way he taught me. "I'll kill you if you ever touch me again. Got that? I WILL KILL YOU!"

I push him back and he only stands there shock-faced, either at what I said or the realization of what he's done. This is the first time he's ever hurt me. I push him again.

"Cal!" a deep voice calls. I turn to see Javier Gerard, my father's best friend and a member of the senate. His eyes are darting back and forth between me and Dad. I wait for Dad to say something, to apologize, but he just stands there frozen. The same way he stood when Mom died.

I reach up and rub my lip. Blood stains my hand. I give

Dad a final glare and rush past Gerard and Margret. Gerard calls after me but I ignore him. The five members of the senate stand at the bottom of the steps and stare at me with mixed expressions. I hate them as much as I hate Dad. It's their laws that make Mary what she is—what her whole family is. *Sin of the fathers must fall to their children.* I disregard them and head for the front door.

I need to tell Mary the truth—that I love her, no matter what my father would have her believe. I should've told her when I had the chance.

I WAKE LYING IN A LOWER BUNK, THE FADING image of my father's angry eyes as I ran from his house still etched into my vision. I try to sit up, but my head and shoulder ache with the effort. I let out a groan and try again.

"Take it easy, Kid," Slim says. I turn my head and see he's sitting on the floor, his back propped up against the other bunk in the cell. He's folding toilet paper into shapes and lining them up in a circle along the floor. I'm not sure where I am. The room is familiar, yet not.

"Where … am … I?"

Slim laughs and rips off another sheet of paper. "You must've hit your head, too. Don't you remember? You're in paradise."

I'm suddenly aware of how dry my throat is. As if I

haven't drunk anything in weeks. I try to move my tongue around, inviting saliva to quench the desert in my mouth. "Paradise?" I croak.

"Yeah … any minute Scarlet Wild is going to bring you a flank steak and a bottle of Chateau Margaux. I bet she's not wearing anything today." His eyes gaze off and a smile creases his face.

Scarlet Wild … Slim … the cell … the Arena. Memories flood back like one horrible tidal wave after another that threaten to make me seasick. I groan again, and Slim barks out another laugh. "Welcome back to the real world, Kid. It's not a pretty one, but it's real."

"I'm thirsty."

"Do I look like a freakin' waitress?"

I turn my head and deliberately look him up and down. He rolls his eyes and gives a grunt as he hoists himself off the floor. Careful not to disturb his figures of toilet paper, he grabs a paper cup off the shelf next to the toilet and fills it from the tap. He hands me the cup. I go to lift my arm but the searing pain returns to my shoulder.

"For crying out loud," he complains, as he lifts my neck and feeds me the water. It's cold, and my tongue welcomes the relief. When Slim pulls away, I hold the moisture in my mouth and swish it around, coating my gums, cheeks, and throat.

"Thank you," I say.

Slim again rolls his eyes and sets the cup down on the

floor next to me. He returns to his space on the floor and rips off another sheet of toilet paper. He begins to fold it.

"What are you doing?"

"I'm building houses for fairies—what does it look like I'm doing?"

"Beats me, I'm new here."

He places his newly folded toilet paper box in the center of his circle and scrutinizes his work. "I, my dear clueless friend, am formulating an attack plan. Unlike some of the bozos here, I actually like to know what I'm doing when I start dancing in a blood bath."

"Your number got picked?" I try again to sit up but pain is my master at the moment.

"I told you to take it easy. You had a freakin' saber-tooth take a chunk out of your shoulder. Frankly I'm surprised you're alive at all. You'll have to share your secret on regeneration. If you haven't noticed, your broken leg is healed."

"Healed?" I strain my head forward and lift my leg. I remember it breaking. I move my hands over my chest and down my rib cage. My ribs are healed too. I have a flashback of an injection right before I was branded CS4521. "Nanorobotics," I say. "Some lady injected me before I came in here to fix my broken rib."

Slim lets out a sigh. "Shoot, I was hoping you had some sort of freak mutation that could heal you. I thought it might keep you alive a little longer. Guess I was wrong."

"How long have I been out?"

"A few days." Slim folds another toilet paper box.

"So you have to fight?"

"Oh, yeah. A bunch of us. The Arena is all into these group battles lately. Over a dozen of us got our numbers called out last night. We have a week to prepare. All those other idiots just hit the benches and started pumping weights, as if that's going to save them. It helps, but it's not going to make you win in the Arena. To win you have to use your brain."

"Go for their weak spots," I say, repeating the words he told me before I took on the saber-tooth.

"Exactly." Slim gives me a smile. He starts to move the various toilet paper figures around again. "You have to discover what your opponent's weak point is and take it out." He flicks one of the structures with his finger and it creates a domino effect. Half of them fall over.

"Trying to plan out your funeral again?" a deep voice asks. I look toward the door to see HW11's dark form standing in the doorway. "You know those shanks won't listen. The minute the gun goes off they'll scurry around like ants when you kick over a hill. It's chaos and blood—all it ever is."

"Well, excuse me for trying to do something smart," Slim says.

HW11 ignores Slim. His brown eyes fall on me. "Can you move yet?"

"A little," I say. "Although my shoulder is still hurting."

HW11 shakes his head. "You're lucky that's all it's doing. You should be dead."

"So I've been told."

"Kid's lucky," Slim says. "The legs up in registration injected him with nanorobotics."

HW11 looks a little puzzled. Maybe he wonders why she did something like that. He probably didn't know I'd come into the compound with a broken rib. "Nice job with the saber-tooth," he says.

"Whoa!" Slim's mouth hangs open in mock expression. "Did the great Bear actually give a compliment?" HW11 shoots Slim a glare so menacing it could make scars bleed. Slim lifts his hands in surrender. "My apologies, O Great One."

HW11 steps back as if he's about to leave, but I sit up. Pain shoots into my shoulder, but I'm able to pull myself into a semi-upright position. "Wait! Bear?"

He pauses, his eyes fixed on me.

"Is that your name?" I ask.

He gives a nod.

"I'm sorry I called you a number before. I didn't mean to make you feel less than human. I figure that's what the numbers are for, right?"

Bear gives me a nod, then turns to Slim. "Get the kid ready." Without waiting for a reply, he leaves. I watch him move down the glass hallway, his shoulders so wide he takes up most of the space.

"You got on Bear's bad side, eh?" Slim asks.

I nod. "I called him by his number."

Slim exaggerates a whistle. "That would do it. The rumor is Bear's the one who started the whole name thing. He didn't like being called a number. He said no matter what he'd done, he was still a human being, and humans have names. He got his name right after he killed a grizzly bear with his bare hands."

"How'd you get your name?"

Slim laughs. "Some peckerwood called me it when I split my pants doing squats in the rec room. You know, on account of my healthy size. He didn't last long in the fights. I think Slaughter got the better of him. There's no beating that monster. The day I face him I think I'll just take my own life. Heaven knows I'd show more mercy than he would."

The look in Slim's eyes tells me he's serious. I can only agree. I'd seen what Slaughter was capable of in the past. I recall friends talking about him like he was some kind of hero, as if his brutality merited reward. If I only I knew then what I know now, I would have set them straight. Slaughter is no hero; he's a killer, a cold, sadistic murderer. I can still hear the sound of Dragon's death echoing in my mind. Why did the game masters force me to hear it? I can never let it go. His death will haunt me forever.

"All right, Kid, Bear wants you ready." Slim grunts as he again heaves himself from the floor. "Do you think you can walk?"

I take a deep breath, not really wanting to move at all. "I can try."

"Good. Because despite all that brain knowledge you have, Bear still wants you to train."

"Train for what?"

Slim shakes his head and helps me to my feet. My legs are shaky, and I almost fall over. Slim holds me straight. I let out a groan, and he barks out a laugh. "You really need to remember where you freakin' are. This ain't some all-expense paid vacation, Kid. You have to earn your keep. To earn your keep, you have to fight. Lucky for you, they gave you a week to train with the rest of us."

"I'm fighting in the group battle?"

"You, me, and the other sorry shanks they announced. Bear told me it was my job to train you. Stick with me, Kid, and I'll teach you how to survive in this hell-zone. Like I said before, it's not all about strength. If you don't use your brain, someone's going to remove it for you."

"So what do we do first?"

"After you start walking, I suggest you put your legs to good use, and we find some grub. No point in burning calories if there's nothin' to burn."

"Is it mealtime?"

"Kid, when you've been in the Arena as long as I have, your stomach starts to form a watch of its own. Right now it's telling me my alarm is about to go off. I like to be at the front of the line. Stick to the back, and you might become a meal for one of Slaughter's goonies, if you catch my drift. Don't make me paint you a picture."

Slaughter's name makes me tense. I remember his one, cold eye staring me down the moment I entered the cafeteria. Even now I recall Bear's warning not to get his attention. But an injured animal always attracts predators.

Walk like a man, Dad says in my mind. I straighten and force myself to walk without Slim's aid. I have to ignore the pain. I have to look strong.

BY THE THIRD DAY OF TRAINING, MY SHOULDER is feeling better. There's still a deep scar that I suspect the nanorobotics won't fix. The tiny robots are probably gone now, anyway. I know they don't hang around forever. Slim calls the mark my initiation scar. He has one that wraps around his calf from a beast fight he had with a jaguar. He wears it proudly, like a trophy. I'm not proud of my scar. It reminds me of the first thing I killed. Or the first thing I *remember* killing. The footage shown at the trial was taken after I killed my father—I don't actually remember doing it. I don't ever want to. I pray I never see the memory.

I follow Slim down the glass hallway toward the rec room. I sneak a glance at all the men gathering on the bleachers waiting for Scarlett Wild to announce tonight's victims. I feel sorry for them. I can see the worry on their faces as they wait for their numbers to be called out. The fear of it must be awful. The one good thing about knowing I'd been selected for the group battle is that I still have four days until I'm forced back into the Arena.

Slim leads us over to a climbing wall. I really don't want to climb the stupid thing again. My shoulder may be healed, but my muscles don't approve of this new regimen. Slim can see the disappointment on my face and launches into his daily lecture.

"How do you expect to win in the fights if you can't even lift your own body weight?"

"I know," I grumble. I completely understand where he's coming from, but Slim talks as though he expects me to continue to survive. What happened with the saber-tooth was a fluke, a lucky fall. Building the strength to lift myself is one thing, being able to kill another human being when the time comes to it is something entirely different.

"This time we're going to race," Slim says. "See if you can beat my fat butt to the top. The loser has to do a hundred sit-ups."

"Can you even do a hundred sit-ups?" I tease, shifting my eyes toward his round belly.

Slim's eyes narrow and he gives me a smirk. "Don't worry about me, Kid. I won't lose."

He launches himself up the climbing wall and is feet above me before I realize I'm just standing there like an idiot. I rush to catch up. My hands find the anchors and I lift myself onto the wall. The muscles in my arms and back complain, not wanting anymore of this abuse. I ignore them and climb. As much as I don't want to scale the wall, I'd rather win than do a hundred sit-ups. I push myself harder.

Hand then foot. Lift then push. I reach the top of the wall and climb onto the platform. I look down, wondering exactly how high off the ground I am.

Slim slaps me on the shoulder. "Start on those sit-ups, Kid."

I groan but do what I'm told. Slim grabs my ankles as I begin attacking my abdomen. At twenty reps, each crunch is agony. I push myself to do more.

"Come on, you can do it. Just fifty more. Don't forget to breathe." Slim tries encouraging me, but I'd rather he just shut up. The last ten feel like each one is a ruthless stab to the gut. *Stab* … suddenly I have a flash of a bloody letter opener in my hand, five stab wounds seeping out blood. Another image fills my mind, my father's lifeless eyes. His stained white shirt. Then flashes from a hovercam momentarily blinding me.

I drop back onto the platform, my back smacking against the metal. I cry out in pain but I'm not sure if it's from the memory of what I did to my father or the last of the sit-ups. I feel sick, bile rising in my throat.

"Kid, you okay?" Slim asks. His voice is low and laced with concern. I shake my head. I'm so tired of the memories, the flashes of horror and the feelings of guilt.

"I don't want to see the blood anymore," I whisper. "I don't want to remember his face. Not that way."

Slim is quiet. He looks around as if checking for anyone lingering too close. How could they be? We're at least fifty feet above the others. Besides, half of them are watching Scarlet Wild and her latest disregard for clothing.

"You wanna talk about it, Kid?" he asks. "Maybe talking about it will help."

"How could it help?" I cover my face with my hands. "It's not going to change what happened—what I did."

"What makes you so sure you did anything?"

"I remember the weapon in my hand. I saw the footage—"

"Screw the footage," he snaps. "You don't think I saw that load of shank? Did you ever wonder why you had a freakin' hovercam zooming through your house in the middle of the night? Or was that a normal thing in your house? I know your daddy was a senator, but come on, Kid, you're smarter than that. Do you actually remember stabbing your daddy?"

I try to think back. I try to imagine myself stabbing him, but I can't. The furthest I can go back is waking to seeing the letter opener in my hand. I see the blood. His face. His eyes. I shake my head. "I woke up, and he was already dead."

"See, I told you that you ain't no killer. You were set up, Kid. I don't know what kind of sadistic shank would throw a kid into a hell like this, but whatever you did must have pissed the crap out of them." Slim sits back and rolls his shoulders. He looks down at the platform as if thinking hard.

Could he be right? Was my father murdered by someone else? I had never allowed myself to believe it because everyone told me I had done it. They proved that I did it. *But had I?* The more I think about it, the more I can recall waking to find Dad already dead. I don't remember stabbing him. I don't even remember seeing him after I followed Mary out of the house that night. *But if I didn't do it, then who? Why would they do this to him—to me?*

"I need to tell someone." I push up, bracing to stand. "I don't belong in here. I need to tell some—"

"Who the hell do you think cares enough to listen? Damn, Kid, you're an offender. You don't have rights. You don't even have a name. You think any of those people that watch this show care if you live or die? This is all just entertainment to them."

"But you said it yourself. I didn't kill him. I'm innocent. That means there's someone out there that killed my father—that killed a senator! They have to be found."

"You're preachin' to the choir." Slim sighs and shakes his head. "Look on the bright side. You now know you're innocent. You know you're not a killer. Now you can stop beating yourself up about it and move on with your life."

"How can I move on with my life when I'm trapped in this place? I wanna go home. I wanna see Mary. Tell her how much I love her. I want to live. There's no life in here. Not for long. Not for me, anyway."

Slim grips my shoulder and pierces me with his dark brown stare. He shakes his head. "The only thing you can do for her and yourself is survive. Got it? You have to survive.

The longer you live, the longer you'll have hope. Who knows? Maybe someone is investigating it. You caused a bit of trouble when they threw you in here. No wonder they tried to kill you off early in the game. But you have to prove them wrong, Kid. You have to fight. Fight and survive."

I absorb his words like dry ground receives the rain. He's right. I'm not a murderer. I have to somehow survive this. But I also have to find a way out. The only way I can find out who killed my father is to get outside. The Arena won't help me.

"Just think," Slim says, stretching his neck from side to side. "If we win this battle, you'll at least get a break. That will give you more time to think this through."

I take comfort from that. Slim had informed me that the victors of the group battle get a four week break from the fights; not only them but also the men of their section. Sure they were assigned tasks like food preparation or sanitation duty, but it was twenty-eight days of not having to worry about your identification number being called out. If we win the group battle, all the offenders in Section One will benefit.

"You ready to climb down?" Slim asks.

I nod, get up, and then help Slim to his feet. I look over at the bleachers. Men are gathered around one of the offenders, patting his back, shaking his hand. He stands proud, but I can see the worry and dread in his face. Maybe he'll come back from the fight, maybe he won't. This is the Arena, after all.

“Do you ever worry you’ll get killed?” I ask.

Slim grunts a half laugh. “Every freakin’ day of my life. But this is what I get. I knew the punishment before I committed my crime.”

I hadn’t thought about it before, but I suddenly realize that Slim would have committed a violent crime to be sentenced here. He seemed so nice, especially how he talked about his mother. It was hard to think of him as a criminal.

“What did you do?”

For a moment he stands, silent, as he looks out over the training room. Then he sighs, long and low as he steps closer to the edge of the wall. “I disappointed my mama is what I did. I hung out with the wrong kind of people. I got caught stealing and was sent to the prison mines. The mines aren’t like it is here. There, you don’t have force fields protecting the weapons. The very tools we used could kill a man.”

Slim pauses and looks down at the men now milling about the rec room. I can see pain in his eyes, as if he were thinking back to how he could have done things differently. I know the feeling. Surprising me, Slim clears his throat and continues. “These two big guys kinda ran the show there, you know? Whatever they wanted they got. We had guards, but they always turned the other way when things happened. My best friend in the mines was a kid named Danny. He’d been thrown in because he had an arson problem. He burnt down a few buildings. Lucky for his sorry case, he didn’t kill anyone. Otherwise, he’d have ended up in here. Maybe it would have been better if he had.”

Slim's shoulders shudder as if he's trying to hold back emotions. I wonder if he's ever told this story to anyone before. I wait, letting him tell it in his own time. He sucks in another deep breath then exhales. Inhales and goes on.

"I found Danny's body at the bottom of a shaft when I returned from a piss break. Those two guys had raped and beaten him. They didn't even bother pulling up his pants. They just threw him down the shaft. The guards called it an accident. Can you believe that shank? An accident!"

Slim's hands are balled into fists, clenching so the veins bulge. "I couldn't get the image of Danny's body out of my head. I had to pay them back for what they'd done. I took my pick axe and I ... I killed them. It was the easiest thing I'd ever done in my life." He gives a half smile, his eyes bone dry. I see no remorse in him, only an emptiness—a pit with a bottom hard as stone. "I do regret that I never got to see my mama's face again. Maybe it's a good thing, I guess. Not sure I could have handled her disappointment in me. Knowing her son grew up to be a killer."

Slim and I stand in silence at the top of the rec room for what seems like forever. It's our own silent oasis in the midst of all that fear. There is emptiness in Slim, as if his soul has left a gaping crater. Murder changes a man, no matter how righteous they may appear. After seeing that emptiness, the horrible, agonizing emptiness in Slim, I make a decision. I will not kill another man. If I do, I'll be no different from everyone else in here. I'll only bind myself to this life forever.

I have to find a way out of this prison. Getting out is the only way back to freedom. To living.

-SEVEN-

THE OFFENDERS ARE IN A GOOD MOOD TODAY. They joke around, and I can almost catch a glimpse of what they were like before being brought to this place. Those of us that will be fighting tonight aren't so jovial. We keep to ourselves and think about how the week has flown by. Slim trained me, even shared his survival plan, but I'm not sure it's enough to keep me alive. A week isn't enough time to prepare my body to fight. I would need months, years, to build up the strength I need.

I don't even bother talking to anyone else but Slim. They all call me Kid when I pass by, but they don't say anything else, as if they don't want to get to know me. A guy in our section I'd only met that day was called to Fight to the Death. He lasted twenty minutes. I didn't watch the show, but the monitor was so loud, I couldn't block out the cheers when he died. I'm glad I didn't get to know him. There'd be too much sorrow for a lost friend. I don't need to feel anymore emotions. I already feel too many.

The monitors in the cafeteria play nothing but the news and repeats of the fights. Right now I see clips of the riots Slim says have been happening since my trial began. The news anchor talks without emotion as an automobile fire blazes behind him. "Vandalism and the destruction of property seem to be the calling card of those shouting to the senate for reform. This is just the latest in an ongoing attempt for equality between true citizens of Primus and those labeled defectors. Senator Javier Gerard addressed the nation earlier this week."

The screen fills with a familiar face, one of my father's closest friends. My first thought is how tired he looks. Shadows, in half circles, rest under his hazel eyes, deepening the lines of aging. He's standing outside the Senate Hall. Behind him, the fifteen pillars of justice, each representing a member of the senate, symbolically signify how the senate supports Primus.

"We ask that those responsible for these crimes come forward," Senator Gerard says into the microphone. "Not to be punished for these actions, but to find restitution from the biases that are causing this outcry. We seek peace and equality among all our citizens, those with or without the blue brand upon their arms."

"Blah, blah, blah," Slim says as he slides onto the seat next to me and drops his over-stacked plate onto the table. "You think if they wanted peace, they wouldn't have marked people with a brand in the first place. Tell that guy to try to find a job with a mark on his arm. You know how many defectors are in the mines? All because they can't find work to buy food, so they had to steal it. All because of this bozo and his ideas of equality."

"Gerard's not like that," I say. "I know him. He's a nice guy."

"Oh yeah? So are half the men in this place until they get a knife in their hand."

"I believe he really does want a better Primus."

"Oh, do you?" Slim points his pinky high into the air as he downs his drink. "Next time he's up for election, let me know and I'll make sure to vote for him. Heck, sign me up to be a part of his campaign."

Cheers ring out and I look up to see two guys in the middle of an arm wrestling match at a table in the middle of the room. While the men shout encouragement to their favorites, I think it's odd to see smiles and laughter in a place so grim.

"I don't blame those shanks for celebrating," Slim says, picking a chicken leg off his plate. "I'd be just like them if I knew I had the night off."

"You've had a whole week off." I roll a grape around my plate with a plastic spork, but I don't eat anything.

Slim sets into his chicken leg, eating it with gusto as if it's his last meal. "It ain't the same. We knew we had a fight coming. That dread never leaves you. Tonight they're lucky."

"I guess."

"What's the matter with you? You haven't eaten a thing. What did I tell you the first rule to survival is?"

"Use your brain?"

Slim drops his barren chicken bone to his plate, picks up another fleshy thigh and points it at me. "Don't get smart with me. Your brain needs fuel too, Kid. Don't eat, and you won't think straight. Why else do you think I eat the way I do? I'm fueling my brain."

I can't help but laugh. Slim looks at me with hard eyes.

"You think I'm being funny?" He tears off a piece of meat with his teeth and chews only twice before swallowing. "Humor will get you nowhere in life. Not in here anyway. In the Arena, life is serious. And I am serious when it comes to food."

"What's the point in eating? The minute I get into the Arena, I'm going to barf it all up. I did last time."

Slim holds up a hand. "Please, don't mention that stuff while I'm eating. It ruins my appetite. Besides, do you want your last meal to be half a grape? Go get some freakin' meat. You need the protein."

"You should listen to your mommy, pretty boy."

I turn around to see Slaughter. His large frame hovers over me, his one bloodshot eye staring me down intensely. Immediately I stiffen. Of all the people in this compound, the last one I want to talk to is Slaughter. Slim doesn't say anything. I know how much he fears the killer. Slaughter looks me up and down, and his tongue flicks across his upper lip.

Nervous hairs lift on my arms as I contemplate what Slaughter wants. I wish for Slim to say something, but he's as frozen as I am. My eyes dart around Slaughter, trying to see if I can find Bear. Maybe if I call to him, Slaughter will go away. The killer notices what I'm doing and moves in closer. He puts his face next to my ear, and I can smell the sweat on his body.

"It gets chaotic in group battles, pretty boy. Anything can happen." His whispered voice sends a bone-chilling wave down my back. Then his words sink in. I never thought to ask Slim whose team we were fighting. Slaughter leans back and examines my face—then a sly smile cracks his lips. "That's right, sweetheart, soon it'll just be you and me. Don't worry, it won't hurt … much. You might even enjoy it."

His fingers brush against my arm in an intimate way. Without thinking, I shove him back. "Get away from me, you dog!"

Slaughter steps back, crashing into an offender's plate. It falls to the ground with a smack. Mashed potatoes spray Slaughter's legs. The offender scurries away as I stand, fists raised. I am suddenly aware that the whole cafeteria has gone still. I imagine they have never seen anyone publicly stand up to Slaughter, let alone a hundred-and-forty-pound sixteen-year-old. His mouth narrows to the point that his lips disappear. His chest flexes. A vein in his forehead pulses, as if trying to break free. I can tell he wants to kill me right here and now. I can almost sense the cameras zooming in, getting the best shot they can.

"You're dead, pretty boy," Slaughter promises. "You just wait. I'm coming for you."

I say nothing but I stand my ground. My father taught me that you never back down from bullies. You have to show them that they can't make you feel inferior.

Slaughter glares at me one last time and marches out of the cafeteria, his angry feet slapping the floor as he goes. The men in the room are still quiet but soon they return to their meals and eventually, their laughter.

I turn to Slim, who's forgotten all about the food on his plate. He's staring up at me like I'm holding a picture of his mother. "That was the bravest-stupidest thing I have ever seen in my life. Are you freakin' nuts?! You know what that guy is going to do to you?"

"You're not going to let him," I say as I sit back down.

"*I'm* not going to let him? How the hell did you pull me into this? That guy makes me want to piss my pants—I think I *did* just piss my pants."

"You said you'd protect me—look out for me."

"I never said I'd take on *Slaughter*! Why did you do that?"

Why did I do that? Most of it was fear. Fear of Slaughter's threats, but mostly fear of not being able to do anything to prevent it. "My father always told me that no one can make you feel less than who you are. The only way is if you allow them to do it. I couldn't let him make me think he had me. I'm not his property. I won't let him touch me. I had to do something. I had to stand up for myself. If he kills me, so what? At least I die like the man my father raised me to be. Not a coward."

Slim's shoulders slump down and he looks away. I can tell my last words stung Slim. I didn't mean to call him a coward, but I had. I'd seen Slaughter bully others in the compound, including Slim, and they all did the same thing—they ignored it. Part of me is angry at Slim for staying still as Slaughter spoke his foul words to me. I try to return to my food, but what little appetite I might've had is gone. Slim seems to have given up on his food too, because he joins me as I stand and clear my plate. In silence we drop our plates in the bin and leave the cafeteria. The men and cameras watch us go.

AN HOUR LATER WE SIT ON THE BLEACHERS, waiting for the program to start. The logo of the Arena fills the screen, and the music trumpets throughout the room. The introduction fades, and Scarlet Wild stands in front of a stone wall. She wears a chainmail bikini with a blood-red sash holding a long saber against her thigh. The offenders cheer, obviously approving of her outfit.

"Tonight we take a journey back through time," Scarlet says, her voice low and oily. "Back to the age of battlements and strongholds, where two armies will collide in a battle the likes of which you have never before seen. Which of our armies will triumph in this war to win the others' ensign?"

"I told you!" Slim shouts. "You bozos said I was full of shank, but I told you! I was right. She gave enough clues in the Choosing."

"Sit your fat crack down," someone shouts from above.

Scarlet begins naming off the offenders that will take part in the battle. Slim sits down and turns to me. "I told you this was what would happen, didn't I?"

I nod. "Now what? It's like Bear said before. They don't listen." I nod toward the other offenders chosen to fight for our section.

"Well, they need to start listening before they get us all killed."

"Slim, every army needs a general. They'll listen to their leader."

"I don't know how to be a leader."

"My dad always said that sometimes you are appointed, but other times you have to take charge. *You* need to take charge."

"You're right!" Slim stands up and marches down the bleacher steps. He takes a position in the center of the blue mat, his posture tall and straight. Some of the men in the room tell him to sit down, but he ignores them. "I need all the men fighting tonight to follow me. I have a plan."

Nobody moves. Some of the men laugh. Slim's resolve doesn't waver while he waits expectantly. I join him on the mat, expecting others to follow my example, but they remain unmoved.

I turn to Slim. "You need to take control."

Anger burns in his eyes. I can almost feel the anger and the reasons behind it—anger for the idiots that can't see past his appearance, anger at the hand he's been dealt in life, anger that the other inmates are willing to risk *his* own life because they're too proud to trust him. Slim marches over to one of the weight sets and pulls a twenty pound ring from the shelf. He stomps back onto the mat and hurls the ring at the screen. It smashes directly between Scarlet Wild's breasts and cracks spread outward. The screen goes black.

"If you want to live, follow me! If you want to die, stay." Without another word, Slim marches out of the rec room and into the training area. I steal a glance at Bear who stands against the wall, a smile on his face. Without waiting for anyone else, I follow behind my general.

"ARE YOU READY?" I ASK, HANDING SLIM HIS broad sword. He takes it with a nod and glances at his reflection on the mirrored wall.

"Stay close to me, Kid. We have more than one enemy out there."

I know what he means. Slaughter will not hesitate to abandon his section to seek me out. I grab the hilt of the slashing knife at my waist. The brass plaque in the weapons room called it a kopis. It's long, slightly curved, and the blade has a dip close to the base. Bear said it was light-weight and best for close combat. I took his advice and ordered it up as one of the five items I was allowed. Bear entered the info on the pad and asked me to name my other items. Slim had made me take a bag of rations. He said it would only be filled with dried meat, nuts, and a flask of water, but that the group battles could go on for hours, maybe days. It all depended on how elaborate the game masters made the challenge.

I also chose leather armor much like Slim's that covered my upper body, a helmet that left my ears exposed, and my trusty halberd. The long staff had proven a smart choice against the saber-tooth, and I couldn't pass it by when I saw a new one in its place. Bear had pushed in the orders and given us all a farewell before leaving us to the mirrored room. The Arena supplied us with knee-length tunics and sandals that laced up to our calves.

Slim leaves my side to stand next to the white pad on the wall. He'll press the button when we're ready. "Listen up, shanks," Slim booms. "You heard what Scarlet said. Each team will have a fortress of some kind, and an ensign. For those of you who flunked grade school, an ensign will be a flag of some sort—a talisman that we need to protect. If Slaughter's team has any brains, they'll be protecting theirs, too. We need to capture Slaughter's ensign to end the battle. I want to know right now who wants to defend and who wants to attack."

I can tell from the wary expressions in the men's eyes that the choice is hard. Some shy away, backing as far as they can against the mirrored walls, muttering under their breath about facing Section Six. Others step forward, anxious to use their weapons. The way they stand, clinging to their knives and swords, reminds me that they're killers. I'm not sure which I'd rather do, defend or attempt to get past Slaughter's men—either way blood will spill.

One offender raises his hand. I don't know his name, but I can tell he's been in the Arena for a while because his face is full of crisscrossing scars. His ginger hair is longer than the others', making him haggard and greasy. His voice is deep and grabs the attention of the others around us. "I'll head up the offense."

"Thanks for volunteering, Fist," Slim says. I can tell he's relieved he didn't have to assign someone. Going to meet Section Six head on would need a person willing to go. "I need seven other men to go with Fist. The other ten will stay with me to help defend the fortress. Now then, who's going with Fist?"

Several offenders raise their hands, but not enough. More of the men seem to be pulling back with those glued to the walls. I lift my hand, but Slim rolls his eyes and shakes his head. Feeling a little dumb for trying, I lower my arm.

"You three!" Slim points at the offenders in the far back. One of them pretends not to have heard, but he's elbowed in the side. The moment his eyes connect with Slim, I know he'd rather be anywhere but here. "You'll all join Fist and those on offense."

The men shrug as if it's nothing to them, but their eyes betray the lie. They're afraid. Their fear is almost contagious. I feel it creeping into my gut, trying to make me panic. I know that if I ever had to face off with any of these men, I'd be dead. Slaughter's sickening stare bursts into my mind. I recall his threat. He wouldn't hold back from keeping his promise, even with all of Primus watching. Maybe I should be afraid.

"All right, you shanks," Slim calls, with a slap to his thigh. "Take a moment to say your prayers to God. If you don't believe in God, I suggest you start now. You'll need him soon." He turns to Fist and whispers something in his ear, and they move closer to the door with the panel.

Some of the men begin to joke around. Others lower their heads, and I can see the silent prayer trembling on their lips. I recall my mother showing me how to pray. She taught me that I didn't always have to kneel, and that God would hear my prayers even if I didn't say them aloud. I wonder now if I should ask for his help. I close my eyes and try to form the words in my mind. A loud growl of a laugh sounds next to me, and I feel the time for reverence has passed.

I pull the kopis blade from the sheath at my side and decide to use the time to practice. I slash the blade up and down, side to side, and the offender behind me laughs. He's tall and thick-faced, his skin a light shade of brown.

"You're swinging that blade all wrong. What are you trying to do, trim bushes?" He takes the blade from me and slashes it through the air a few times. "Don't twist your wrist or you lose power in the strike, use your elbows instead. Use your wrists to guide the strike. Also target the exposed areas—like this." He swings the blade and it comes within inches of my neck. A smile crosses his ugly face, and he hands the kopis back. "Try it that way."

I follow his instructions and I'm amazed at the difference. Without turning my wrist, I have way more control of it. It feels more like an extension of my arm rather than an awkward tool. "Hey, thanks! What's your name?"

"I don't have a name. You know that. The Arena took it from me. You can call me Hammer. Everyone else does."

"Do you like to fight with a hammer or something?"

He laughs. "No. It's because my face is as flat as the backside of a nail." He turns his head to the side and I inspect his very flat nose and forehead. He gives a smile, but it doesn't add any roundness to his features at all. "A face only a mother could love, right?"

"I guess."

He booms out a laugh. "No one likes an ugly face. Just doesn't sit well with them. I'll be defending the fortress with Slim—stick with me, Kid, and I'll make sure no one gets the better of you."

I give a nod. Hammer slaps my back and we turn just in time to see the pad on the wall glow red. My stomach tightens as Slim smacks his hand down. The door whooshes open, and I step toward the conveyer.

HEAVY RAIN POUNDS ONTO THE STONE WALL AS we jump from the lift's platform. Part of me wants to rush out into the downfall and bathe myself in it. Although I know it's not real rainfall, it reminds me of freedom, of a world outside the walls of the compound. Slim brings me back to reality, shouting for those of us defending the fortress to follow him. He orders the others to go with Fist.

The stone wall is wide and connects to a much larger structure at least three stories high. There are no windows or doors. It's just a tall block of stone bricks. A rushing river, at least twenty yards wide, splashes at the base of the fortress, and two wooden bridges with thick chains link the stone structure to a craggy field beyond. Lightning flashes, and I glimpse another fortress in the far distance.

I marvel at the grandeur of the colosseum. I recall from my history classes that the construction was based off another building lost to time but only a fraction of the size of this. I wonder briefly if they held such battles inside or if it was used for something else.

Fist shouts orders, and he and his men march down one of the bridges and are soon lost in the stormy murkiness. I turn to Slim who has found the ensign, a tall golden eagle mounted at the top of a thick brass pole. It glimmers, almost radiating with power.

"We defend the Eagle, men," Slim shouts above the storm. "I need three of you on look out." He points to three offenders. "I want one of you at each end of the wall and the third—keep your eye on the field. The second you spot anything—shout."

Slim turns to Hammer. "I need you and three more to defend the bridges. Two per bridge. Don't let anything pass."

"I'm not lettin' anything through. You can bet on that," Hammer says. I want to volunteer to take the bridge, but Hammer looks past me and chooses three much larger, more experienced men to fight with him. I don't blame him. I'm not strong, and I'm small. They are better fit to defend the bridges. I still feel like a loser, the last one picked on the team at school.

"You other three will stand with me," Slim says. "We're the Eagle's last defense. You will also be carriers for me, delivering orders to the other men. Should I fall, you are to take orders from Kid."

"What?" I ask.

"You heard me," he shouts. "You know the attack plan."

The other men nod in agreement and turn to face the field. Thunder booms overhead and is followed by the roar of cheers from the spectators somewhere beyond the rain.

I tighten my grip on my halberd and focus on the distant fortress. I hate that I don't know what's happening. Slim was smart to take the fight to them. Section Six is used to throwing their weight. They won't expect us to make the first move.

"How will we know when their ensign is captured?" I ask.

"Usually a trumpet will sound. It's a signal that the fight is over. But don't trust the men to stop fighting because of it. Especially those men."

"What do you mean? Won't they know they've lost?"

"Remember, Kid, this isn't a game. This is life in the Arena. It's always a fight to the death. They may lose their ensign, but I expect they'll keep going until they've killed us—or we've killed them."

Dread weighs on me. Slim's right. I keep forgetting what this place is. It's not about sportsmanship or who captures whose ensign. It's about killing. I shudder as I think of Slaughter. I know he's out there, planning my death. My muscles tense, and I struggle to ignore the cold that seeps into my skin.

A watchman cries out a warning before three burly men charge the left bridge. Hammer shouts a war cry and meets them with his broadsword swinging. It's a clash of metal on metal that leaves my ears ringing. My heart races and I dart a look at Slim, whose brow is set in fierce determination.

"Hold the bridge!" he orders. "Hold the bridge!"

Hammer takes down one of the men with a slash to the gut but another is on him at once. Our other bridge guard falls and his killer charges toward us. The two men beside me rush toward him, sword and battle-axe raised to kill. They meet in the center, and it's a swift execution. They join in the fight with Hammer, and the other man is laid to the ground.

"I had him!" Hammer shouts. "You shanks get back."

Another watchman sounds a cry, but it's cut off. I glance over my shoulder in time to see him fall over the side of the wall, an arrow in his chest.

"Arrows!" Slim shouts. The other men ready their shields—but I don't have one. I opted for the spear instead. I hunch down behind the wall hoping it will give me the shelter I need. I hear whistles whiz through the air and another cry of pain. Another bridge guard is down.

"Hammer," Slim shouts. "Find that archer!"

"Already on it!"

I hear more whistles and a few arrows clatter to the stone floor. I risk a peek over the wall and see Hammer swinging his broadsword. The archer falls back but releases an arrow that lodges in Hammer's thigh, just above the knee. Hammer continues to stomp forward. Two slashes of his sword and the archer lies motionless. Hammer relieves the man of his weapons and turns toward the fortress.

"There's someone behind you!" a watchman shouts.

Hammer lifts his sword but quickly lowers it. "Fist!"

Despite the rain, I can see blood covering him. Hammer staggers to him and helps pull his comrade to the bridge. The other two men take Fist from Hammer and carry him across the bridge. They set him down at Slim's feet and Hammer limps toward us as the other two men return to guarding the bridge.

"What happened to the others?" Slim asks.

Fist shakes his head. "Dead. They're all dead."

"How many of Slaughter's men are left?"

"Not sure. We took out plenty, but they had archers on the wall. Slaughter guards their Eagle. They also cut down one of their bridges. It's heavily defended."

Slim straightens, taking stock of our men. There are only nine of us left. I try to silence the skeptic in my mind, but I don't know how we're going to win. How can nine of us defend the Eagle and face off with Slaughter?

“I need food,” Slim says.

“What the hell are you talking about,” Hammer growls. “We’re in the middle of a battle, and you want to eat?”

“It helps me think, all right?” I pull the ration bag from my shoulder and hold it out to him. He tears into the dried meat and paces the length of the wall. His eyes keep darting to the backside of the fortress. Two more paces, another swallow of meat, and he grins. “I got it. Hammer, I need you to take down one of our bridges. That’s brilliant thinking on their part. One is easier to defend than two. Hammer and Fist, you are now in charge of leading the defense.”

“Us,” Fist asks. “What about you?”

“Me and Kid are going to get their Eagle.”

“What?” I shout. “They have at least ten men, and Slaughter has to count as three. How do you expect us to fight them?”

Slim laughs. “I don’t. We’re going to steal it right out from under ’em.”

-NINE-

SLIM LEADS US ALONG THE FAR EDGE OF THE field. His plan is to try to take their fortress from the rear. I'm not entirely sure how he expects to do that, but I don't feel I have much choice but to follow. It's either wait for Slaughter to come to us, or we go to him. At least we're moving forward. Dad would like it. He hated standing idle. *True leaders walk forward with determination, no matter the cost.*

Rain soaks the ground, making the thick mud stick to my shoes like hungry leeches. It squelches into my sandals and coats my toes in its grime. Like Slim, I tear into the dried meat, letting the rain help soften the bits of leather, giving me a little energy before the final push forward. Lightning flashes in the fake sky, followed by a tremendous boom. I wonder for a moment if it's safe to be out in the open during a thunderstorm but remind myself the lightning isn't real—*or is it?* I can imagine the game master finding delight in electrocuting the offenders.

We make it to the head of the river. I know we are against the wall of the fighting ground, but the illusion of the

Arena makes the water appear as if it's coming from a mountain side. I step in closer and the trickery flickers. For a moment I can make out a huge pipe spurting the water out. I cringe. Slim's plan is crazy. We might drown before we even make it to the back of Slaughter's fortress. Slim pulls the red cape from his shoulders and drops it to the mud with a slap.

"Help me take this armor off," he calls above the rain and rush of the river. I quickly undo the lacing at his side as best as I can in the gloomy light. Once it's loosened he pulls it off and tosses it to the ground before motioning for me to raise my arm so he can unlace mine. "It will make things easier without the added weight. Here," he hands me one end of armor cording. "Tie it around your wrist. I don't want us separated. We jump in and get to the other side, no matter what. Use your knife to help you get a grip on the shore but don't cut yourself—or me."

I nod in agreement, tie the end of the cape around my wrist, and pull the kopis from the leather sheath at my hip. I wonder if I should have brought the halberd. The staff might have helped to move through the water better than a curved knife. *Too late now.*

Slim checks the strap across his chest holding the quiver and bow we took from the fallen archer, then turns to me. He doesn't say a word, but I know he's waiting for me to say I'm ready. I'm not sure I'll ever be ready. We could drown. If we don't drown, we have no protection and our only weapons are two knives, a bow and a quiver of arrows. I'm not even sure Slim knows how to shoot an arrow. I certainly can't. This could be the dumbest decision we've ever made. Then again, if we succeed, it will be brilliant.

"I'm ready," I lie, giving Slim the go-ahead. He nods and leaps into the river, with me a second behind.

The water covers my head, deafens me. Its frigid bite is like a thousand needles in my skin. I forget to exhale as I go down and water rushes up my nose, stinging my sinuses. I kick my legs, but the current pulls me down. Down and down and no amount of kicking moves me upward. The ache for air burns my lungs, and the surface is so far away.

The leather strap around my wrists tightens as Slim tugs on it, but it's as though I'm caught in a sick game of tug-of-war—and I'm the rope. The water grips my waist, yanking me downward until my leg scrapes across a rough floor. With all the strength I have, I push off and finally break free of the current. Slim has a firm grip on the cording, and doesn't relent as he pulls me, hand over hand toward him. I cough, freeing the water from my lungs and suck in delicious air.

"Swim!" Slim shouts. He pulls me closer to the shoreline until I'm able to stab my kopis into the thick mud and haul myself up onto the bank. With my energy now wasted, I collapse into the mud. It hurts to breathe yet I take wonderful, life-giving breaths over and over. I roll over and let the rain pelt against my skin, warming me. "No time to rest, Kid. We've got to move."

I climb to my knees and push off the muddy ground. Slim sprints ahead. I have no idea how a man so large can move so fast. I push myself to catch up. Slaughter's fortress comes into view, and we slow our pace. Hopefully no one is guarding the rear. No way to know until an arrow strikes me.

Every step we take feels like an awful game of Russian roulette. All it would take is one of Slaughter's men to look down. My pounding heart sounds like a thousand soldiers marching; so loud it could give us away if it weren't for the rain. Thick mud slathers the ground around the fortress. Every sticking step I take saps more and more of my failing energy. Step, pull, plop, step, pull, plop. I pray no one hears my laboring footsteps over the downpour. The cacophony blends steps, heartbeat, and pounding rain, forming a symphony of terror.

Miraculously, we make it to the wall, and Slim signals for us to hurry toward its center. Part of me feels safer. Slaughter's men would have to look directly over the wall to see us now. Doubt creeps into my mind, telling me this is hopeless, that at the top of this wall is a man who has killed hundreds of others with no reservations. What if I am faced with having to kill another just to save myself? Can I kill another to stay alive?

"Now we climb," Slim says while I survey the slick cement wall. "You can do this. It's not any different than what we've been doing all week. Once we get to the top, you grab their Eagle and jump back in the river. Let it take you downstream a bit, then get out and run as fast as you can back to the others."

"What about you? Fist said Slaughter was—"

"Forget that! All you have to do is get the Eagle. Leave whoever is guarding it to me. Come on, I'll race you to the top."

"Last one up has to do a hundred sit-ups," I say with a laugh.

"You're on." Slim flashes me a smile and launches up the wall. I marvel that he can climb so effortlessly while I carefully choose the stones that stick out far enough to offer purchase. I lift myself from the mud and follow up after him. I try to keep the negative thoughts from clouding my focus. I know who waits for me at the top. Who Fist said guarded the Eagle. I know what Slaughter's capable of, and what he'll do to me if he gets the chance. Slim might've sounded brave, but I saw the fear in his eyes.

My legs scream for me to stop, but I didn't come this far, survive the water, the mud, and the rain, to let them fail me now. I grab another stone and pull myself higher. The stones are slippery, and my mud-coated sandals don't help. Like an idiot, I look down—and wish I hadn't. Vertigo grips me, and I have to rest my head against the stone and wait for the dizziness to pass. *You can do this. You can make it to the top.*

Lightning flashes, and the fortress rocks with thunder. I hold on. Slim slips down a few feet but manages to stop himself. I'm ahead of him now. If only this was the rec room, and the penalty for being last was just sit-ups. I wait for Slim to catch up, and we make it to the top side by side. Slowly, silently, we pull ourselves over the wall.

The silver Eagle stands three feet away, gleaming in the gray. I try to test the weight of it in my mind, wondering if I can hoist such a heavy object and escape with it. Only three feet to the Eagle and at least another ten feet to the wall. If I can manage to get there before anyone notices, I might get far enough down river that their arrows can't reach me. No guards are near, and while I can hear Slaughter ordering the men about, he sounds far away.

Slim unslings the bow from his back. He nocks an arrow and mouths, "Now."

With my heart racing like never before, I dart to the Eagle and lift up the brass staff. It's lighter than I imagined and comes out of its base with ease. I take one step toward the wall and a loud ringing fills the air. The shock of it makes me drop the Eagle. It clatters to the ground and I rush to pick it up.

"They've got the Eagle!" Slaughter shouts.

I lift the Eagle and run. *Ten feet to the wall.*

Something whooshes past my ear. Men scream. Slim roars. I run.

Five feet. Three.

I climb onto the wall and an arrow pings off the Eagle.

"Jump!" Slim shouts. "JUMP NOW!"

I don't hesitate. I throw myself from the wall and crash into the water below. Instantly the current has me, pulling me from the fortress. I kick my legs until my head breaks the surface. Arrows whiz around me, but over it all, the rushing water, the thrumming rain, and the ringing alarm, I hear a howl of rage.

Twisting myself in the water, I see Slaughter on the wall, a sword in each hand. Lightning flashes behind him, making him appear more ravenous demon than man. His war cry cuts through the cold water and sends a shiver down my spine.

I check the river for Slim but I don't see him. "Slim," I shout, trying to be heard above the noise. "Slim!"

My head falls under the water as I fight against the current. I have to find him. I have to make sure he made it. I fight for the surface again, cough and shout for my friend. But I see no sign of Slim. I've beaten Slaughter, but at what cost?

The fortress fades away, the murky light and rain sweeping it from view. A loud slurping sound rises above the tumult, but I only see the river continuing forever through a vast field. I know it's just an illusion, what the game masters want me to see, but I feel the pull that grabbed me earlier. I want to drop the Eagle, but now I cling to it as if it's my life preserver. I resist the force that threatens me, fight it with all my strength, but it's useless. The current is too strong and sucks me ever closer, to what I wonder: another pipe? A waterfall? A spinning blade? Anything is possible with the madmen running this house of horrors.

The field vanishes, and I see the wide mouth of a pipe, with the number fifty emblazoned above it. I'm not given a chance to think about its significance as I rush toward the opening. I take one last searching glance for Slim before the water pulls me into darkness.

My head remains above water as I'm swept so swiftly through the tunnel that air blows against my face. I realize then that I am out of danger—at least from Slaughter's men. I got the Eagle, and I didn't have to kill anyone. A cry of triumph bursts from my mouth, and the pipe bends sharply to the right. *I won!* And I'm still not a killer. The Arena hasn't made me one, yet.

A dim green light fills the tunnel, emanating from a small sign that says *Emergency Exit*. Below it is an airtight door with a circular wheel affixed to it. As the waters rushes me past, I brush the grooves in the cement used as a ladder. Too soon, I'm beyond the exit and while I fight the current to get back to the door, it's useless. The exit's behind me now, but I know a secret. One I don't plan to forget.

Another bend in the pipe forces me down into the water. Just as I break free of the surface, the pipe brightens with the dim light of the Arena. Before I know it, I'm thrown from the pipe and somersaulted into the river. The pressure threatens my grip on the staff, but I squeeze tighter. I will not let go of the Eagle.

I make no effort to swim forward, only to float along with the pull of the river. I close my eyes and see the green words imprinted on my eyelids. *Emergency Exit.*

Water splashes over my face and I open my eyes. Our fortress is in view and I begin swimming toward the shoreline. The rain has stopped, and a brilliant sun warms the sky. I grab hold of the bank and use the Eagle's staff to hoist me onto land. Achingly, I climb out from the river, slipping and sliding along the bank. I lose my footing and almost fall back in when a hand grabs my arm. Fist's scarred face creases with a mostly toothless smile as he helps me to my feet.

Cheers sound from the invisible spectators as I drag the Eagle behind me. Hammer and the others applaud as I approach the bridge. I search for Slim, but I don't see him.

"Where's Slim?"

Fist shakes his head. "He hasn't come back."

I turn and check the field, then the river, but he's not there. *Where is he? Where?*

Fist grabs the Eagle, gives me a hard slap on the back, and holds the ensign high over his head. The offenders around us cheer as a trumpet sounds throughout the colosseum. The spectators roar with enthusiasm. We've won the group battle.

I don't cheer with the others. I walk forward toward the open field, see the carcasses of the fallen men. Men with no names, only numbers. Their blood mixes with the mud, turning the wet ground red. This is no victory. These men died trying to survive. But for what? Another day in the Arena? Another day in this hell?

"SLIM!" I shout to the empty field.

The men look at me like I've lost it, and maybe I have. Maybe they can hear the pain in my voice, the longing for my friend. I shut my eyes and see once again the green glow of the exit sign. There's no true survival in the Arena. You live one day only to die another.

I know what I have to do.

-TEN-

"HEY, KID, THE EXIT'S THIS WAY," HAMMER calls out. I ignore him and continue to walk past the line of dead offenders. The mud grabs hold of my sandals, threatening to pull them from my feet. I hate this place, the mud, the invisible crowd—everything. I pull the kopis from my belt and slash the leather straps holding up my sandals. I throw them up to the sky. Mud rains down and the sandals and kopis fall into the mud, vanishing forever. I drop to my knees and stare out across the field.

In the distance, Slaughter's fortress rises dark and foreboding, but there's no sign of anyone moving about. Not that I can see, anyway. I wait, hoping I'll spot Slim's large frame moving out in the field, but there's only mud.

"All offenders are to return to their sections," a monotone voice blares through a loudspeaker. I turn back to our stronghold and see the surviving offenders in my section helping the wounded onto the lift. Our once triumphant ensign now lies in the mud, its golden majesty mixing with the blood of the fallen.

I want out. I want out so bad it's tearing me apart inside. I charge the Eagle and yank it from the ground, then throw it as hard as I can toward the field.

"I'm innocent!" I yell. "I didn't kill my father!"

"ALL OFFENDERS ARE TO RETURN TO THEIR SECTIONS."

"You don't own me!" I scream at the sky. "I'm innocent!"

Murmurs shudder through the crowd. Are they listening? Do they care? Or now that the fight is over, do they just return to their everyday lives? Why should they get to leave while I have to stay?

"Kid," Fist shouts. "Come on."

The lift lowers again, but I'm not getting back on it. I'm not going to let them put me back in my cage just to make me fight again. "I haven't killed anyone. I don't belong here."

"CS4521, YOU ARE TO RETURN TO YOUR SECTION."

"My name is Calvin Sawyer! Call me by my name!"

The sun vanishes and the Arena plunges into darkness. It's utterly silent. I hear no spectators, no offenders, no rushing water. I hold my ground, waiting for the game masters to strike me down with lightning or some vicious beast they've concocted in a laboratory. They might be the gods of this world, but I will defy them to my very last breath. I count the seconds as they turn to minutes.

A brilliant beam of light blasts me in the face, shocking my eyes. Then another. I hear the slapping and squishing of boots marching toward me through the thick mud. With fists clenched, I wait. I may not kill, but I will fight.

It doesn't take long before I'm surrounded by at least a dozen guards. Their faces are masked with mirrored shields, so all I see is me. For a fraction of a second, I think that Dad would be proud of me, standing up like this. Funny how I finally might have earned his pride when it's the end of my life. Each guard holds a baton, thick as my arm and black as night. *Are they going to beat me to death? Is that the penalty for speaking out? For wanting freedom—freedom I deserve?*

"You have great resilience, CS4521, I will give you that, but your behavior is lacking. I expected more from the son of a senator." My eyes lock with a woman behind the line of guards—the same woman who branded the identification number into my skin. The guards part their line just enough to let her step through, crimson galoshes leaving a trail of messy gashes in the mud. She moves in close, narrowing her eyes, scanning me up and down. Her arms are folded in a disappointed fashion, as if I am a toddler throwing an embarrassing tantrum. I catch a name badge hanging from the lapel of her white lab coat. *Katherine Marsh, Arena Director.* Beneath her coat she wears a dress that is crimson—the color of blood.

"I didn't kill my father," I say. "I didn't kill him, and I want out."

Her lips curve up in that strange smile she gave me when we first met. "I thought you understood the way things work around here, CS4521. You are an offender. You do not have the right to want anything."

"Didn't you hear me? I said I didn't kill my father. Someone else did. You need to let me out so I can figure out who did it and stop them before they kill someone else."

"CS4521, you do not—"

"Calvin! My name is Calvin!"

"No. You do not have a name, you have an identification code. You are an offender. You have no allegiance. No rights. No hope. You lost that the second you arrived here. You want out? Offenders have only one way out of the Arena."

She motions to the guards, and they all raise their batons, ready to strike. My hands shake, but I stand tall, just the way my father stood when facing the people of Primus. Why won't she listen? Why won't anyone listen? I know behind each mask is a human—someone with emotions, with life. Why can't they see me the same way? "You can kill me, but know you'll be killing an innocent man."

Katherine's smirk turns into a full-blown smile. Her teeth are flawlessly white against her blood-red lips. "Don't you think I already know that?"

Time seems to stop for a moment as her words seep into my mind. Then my vision is blackened by the guards' blows. I see a flash of the director's smile, like a Cheshire cat floating in the dark, before I sink to the ground. Sparks of light fire behind my eyes, and I feel myself shutting down, turning numb. But one thought surfaces before I go to sleep … *I am innocent.*

"PHIL, OPEN THE GATE!"

"I'm sorry, Cal, I can't. Marsha just called and said your father's confined you to the grounds."

What? Now I'm a prisoner? I grab hold of the tall iron gate and yank on it. It doesn't even wiggle. I kick at it, again and again.

"Cal, take it easy," Phil says, pulling me back. "I'm responsible for this gate you know."

My shoulders slump. "I'm just—he just … Did Mary come through?"

"The blonde girl? Yeah. We had a car take her home."

I shake my head and turn back to the house. Phil asks if I'm okay, but I ignore him. There isn't anything he can do about it anyway. My father outranks every man I know. How do you get someone like that to listen to anyone? Instead of going in the house, I walk around back to the gardens Mom spent years on. She loved anything that grew in soil—even weeds, as long as they stayed where she wanted them.

If she were still around, Dad wouldn't be so high strung. She had this way of calming him whenever he lost his temper, or something about the senate was bothering him. She calmed me, too.

I make my way to a pergola Mom insisted Dad help build. The wood is in need of a new finish, but it still looks nice. I sit down in one of the cushioned chairs and try to catch a glimpse of the stars between the wooden beams overhead. I remember the nights we spent as a family hunting for shooting stars or lost heroes in the constellations. Those memories are so long ago, they've almost faded to nothing.

I hear footsteps and look down the path leading to the house. I expect to see Dad, coming to apologize, but it's not him. Of course it's not him. It's only Gerard. Like the unofficial uncle that he is, he's obviously come to help smooth things over between me and Dad. He's like that. He did the same when Mom died and I blamed Dad for it. As if it were his fault she got sick in the first place. At the time, I thought since he was responsible for keeping harm out of Primus, and that included illness. I'd been a fool then, but I wasn't wrong about this. The way he treated Mary wasn't right at all.

"Hey there, buddy boy," Gerard says. "Do you mind if I have a seat?"

I shrug and he sits down next to me. He sets a bottle and two shot glasses on the small table next to his chair, then lifts his long legs up onto the ottoman. He stretches back and groans out a sigh. "Oh, this place brings back good memories. I don't remember the last time I just laid back and looked up at the stars. It's funny how you can forget something so beautiful exists when it's always there."

I grunt. Tonight I can't find beauty in the stars. Right now they're just white dots against a black backdrop.

"You know, Cal, what your dad did tonight was ugly. And you're probably thinking that you'll never forgive him—"

"Got that right."

"—but before you go off all halfcocked, you need to know the pressure he's under. I know he doesn't tell you about work, but there's things you should know about. Don't go blabbing I told you—I swore an oath when I became a senator—but there's rumor of an uprising, and it's got him plain worn out."

"What do you mean?"

Gerard sighs and strokes his chin. "I can't go into the details of it, except that your girlfriend might be involved."

"She would never—"

"Not her, but her kind."

"You mean the defectors?" I sit up. "Gerard, you have to know she's not like that. Neither are her parents. They're good people."

"I know, I know." He waves it off like an annoying fly. "I trust your judgement, Cal. I know you would never get involved in anything shady. You're a good kid and the best judge of character I know—all traits that will make you a fine senator one day."

Now he sounded like Dad. I don't want to be a senator. I don't want anything to do with the government. Dad just wants a successor, someone to carry on his name. He probably wishes he had another son to take his place, someone willing to give up everything for Primus, and that just isn't me.

Gerard sits up and shifts his chair so he's almost knee-to-knee with me. He leans forward and whispers, "Look, the senate has been getting threats, rather strong threats. Our intelligence has confirmed they're coming from an organized branch of defectors. Many are upset about things your dad and I have been trying to change—not the changes themselves, but the speed at which we're working. We both want equality between our groups. We want the blue brand to go away. Unfortunately many in the senate, mostly Senator Lindt and Billings, are not so willing to let some issues go." He leans in even closer, and lowers his voice to little more than movement on the wind. "I don't believe all the threats have come from the blue brands. I believe some of the threats, particularly the ones made against your dad, have come from members of the senate."

A breeze blows up my back, causing the hairs on my arms to stand on end. I knew some of the members often disagreed with Dad, but I never imagined they'd dare to threaten him. "Why would they do that?"

"Because your dad is the senate's consul. He's got a narrow rope to walk. He not only has to keep peace between the citizens, but also the members of the senate. That's what tonight's dinner was all about. The senators your dad asked over are those opposing the end of the blue brand. He's trying to smooth things over with Lindt, Billings, and Watson." Gerard gets up from his chair and stretches his back. He sighs and continues. "I guess what I'm getting at is, try putting yourself in your dad's shoes. You have five senators who are very much against ending the ban on defectors, and you find out your son's dating one of them—and she's here, right now, in your house. How would you feel? Think about it."

I start to interrupt, but Gerard silences me with a wave. "Yes, what he did was wrong. It was truly ugly. But you have to see his side. If any of those senators see him showing support toward a defector right now, he could be accused of being a prejudiced leader and lose all that we've worked for in bringing equality to Primus. Government is a twisted game, Cal. Your dad can't play if you bind his hands behind his back."

I look away from Gerard and stare down at the brick floor, the lines zigzagging this way and that. I had no idea Dad's life was so complex. He's been a senator since before I was born, and he never let on to the stress involved. The most stress I deal with is trying to keep up with my studies.

"He's never hit me before," I mumble, still rubbing the tingle from my cheek. "I didn't even know he had it in him."

Gerard places a hand on my shoulder and squeezes. "He wasn't himself tonight. Sometimes we wear different masks. Tonight you saw one of his uglier ones." He pauses and I follow his gaze to the bottle on the table. "Cal, I've been there for you when your mom died, even when you hit puberty and you were concerned about your voice jumping up and down like a jackrabbit."

We both laugh. He picks up the bottle, and I glimpse the label—whiskey.

"I'll always be here for you," he says as he unscrews the cap. "And this too shall pass. Now. How about we shrug it off with a little elixir?"

"Dad'll kill me if I—"

"Nonsense. He won't even know. Remember, this conversation is confidential. That includes a little sip of fire water. Besides, you look like you could use a drink."

Gerard sits back down and pours two shots. He hands me a glass, and I examine its contents. The liquid is golden brown and has a strong phenolic smell. Having never even sipped alcohol before, I hesitantly press the glass to my lips.

"Whoa, there, buddy boy. Every first drink requires a toast." He lifts his glass and gives me a wink. "I say, here's to your future."

"To my future," I repeat.

"Best thing to do is just open your throat and let it go down fast."

I do as instructed and the taste of whiskey dominates my mouth. I cough and let the burn settle into my stomach, slowly seeping into my blood stream. Gerard laughs and slaps my leg.

"Not bad for your first shot. You have the makings of a natural alcoholic."

I stifle a burp and hold out my glass for more. Gerard smiles and fills it up.

-ELEVEN-

I BLINK SEVERAL TIMES BUT THE BLACKNESS still surrounds me. I can't tell if my eyes are even open, so I reach up to feel for my eyelids. My muscles protest, sending shooting pains up my arms and into my shoulders. I'm lost for a moment, trying to place myself in the here and now. The last thing I remember is the group battle, the rain, the mud, the beating from the guards. I let my index finger glide over the smooth surface of the floor. I know I'm not in the Arena, so where?

I force my hand upward, and moan with the effort. My eyelids are open. I'm either blind or being punished. I imagine the director's sadistic voice telling me that as an offender, I've also lost the right to see. Add it to the many things they've taken from me. I imagine soon, I'll even be denied the right to breathe.

At first I think I'm tied to the floor, but find it's only my injured muscles refusing to move. I slowly flex and extend each limb, listening to the stretching of muscle and the popping of joints. The pain is excruciating, but I bear it. I'm still wearing the short tunic I wore in the group battle. The smell of it and my unwashed body reminds me of the fighting. The sweat. The blood.

Then I remember Slim.

He never made it back, and it's my fault. He died because of me. Slaughter and the others had no idea that we had even penetrated their fortress. We had enough time to grab the Eagle and jump into the river, but I messed that up. Had I not dropped it, Slaughter wouldn't have even known we'd been there until it was too late to react. Now it was too late for Slim.

As an offender of the Arena, I suppose I don't have the right to friendship either.

Wanting to punish myself, I push off the floor and get to my feet. The pain is horrible. I almost cry out but quickly silence myself. Not because someone might be listening, but because I deserve this pain. This and more for what I've done to Slim.

I feel my way to a wall. Like the floor, it's smooth and cold to the touch. I follow it a few feet and find a corner. I follow that wall and soon find another corner, and another. My shin smacks into something, and I fall forward, my knees screaming in pain as they find the hard floor. I reach out and find the object I tripped over with my hands. It's affixed above the floor and sticks out a couple feet. I'm not sure what it is until my hands find water resting in a bowl. It's a toilet.

I double check each wall, searching for a door, a hinge, anything to let me know there is a possible way out of this black box. I find nothing but cool, smooth walls, not even a door. After a while I abandon my efforts and slump down in one of the corners of the room. There's no reason to open my eyes, doing so only strains them—so I sit and I think.

I think about how stupid I was for asking to be let out. How pathetic I must've sounded to the other men in my section. It was just that, for a split second, I forgot who I was—an offender. I expected someone to listen because I hadn't committed a crime. I saw that exit sign, and I wanted more than anything to go through it and return to my life outside the Arena. I wanted to forget that all of this had even happened in the first place.

Don't you think I already know that? Katherine's voice haunts my mind, her question repeating over and over. If she knows I'm innocent, why am I still here? What good comes from me being locked away? Is the person who killed my father somehow connected to the director of the Arena? Is that why I was assigned to fight a saber-tooth just hours after coming here? If so, why did she inject me with the nanorobotics? Why keep me alive at all?

I wish Slim were here. I wish Mary were here. I wish … I wish … I wish.

THE BEAT OF MY HEART THRUMS IN MY ears, almost drowning out the symphony of other sounds. I slowly slide across the park bench until our hips are touching. A breeze blows through the maple trees, and I lean in, breathing in the sweet scent of her perfume. The sun is setting, and we should both be heading home, but I need just another moment with her—a moment to build the courage to try to kiss her for the first time.

"Cal, we should—"

I press a finger on her lips, wishing I was daring enough to place my lips there instead. Mary is the most amazing girl I have ever met in all my life. She's kind, smart, beautiful. I don't want her to tell me it's time to go—I know that already—I just want time to stop.

Her hand touches mine and lingers. I take in a breath, then go for it. Millimeters away from our lips touching, she turns her head, cutting me off. I'm not sure what to do now. My hand feels awkward holding hers. I must have screwed something up. Maybe I talked too much, or didn't talk enough. I thought a date in the park would be romantic, but what did I know about romance?

"I'm sorry, Cal." She speaks in a whisper, and I'm afraid of what she might say. I don't want her to tell me that I'm not the guy for her when clearly we're incredible together.

I'm not sure why I say it, but I do. "Mary, I like you."

Waiting, I tense up slightly as if I just placed my heart on the ground for her to stomp on.

"I like you too, Cal. A lot." She hesitates and I wait for her to give me the crushing blow. There's something wrong with me, I'm sure. A girl like Mary can get any guy she wants. She lets go of my hand and begins fidgeting with the buttons on her sleeve. Before I know it, she yanks her sleeve up, revealing the blue brand stamped on her forearm.

Five arrows under the brand mark her as a fifth generation defector.

"I'm sorry. I should've told you before, but you asked me out, and I really wanted to be with you." She pauses and the orange sky glints in her moist eyes. "I don't want you to get into trouble."

I take her hand and hold it tightly in mine. "You think I care about that? Screw the edict."

"Cal, you could get in trouble. Your father—"

"My father doesn't care what I do. I hardly ever see him to begin with. What I do care about is you." I cup her jaw with my free hand and pull her in close. This time she doesn't pull away. Our lips connect, and a flood of emotions barrels through me. I feel alive and excited. Something wet touches my cheek and I pull back. She's crying.

"I'm I really that bad?"

"No, Cal, of course not. I just—" Her hands cover her face in embarrassment. "I feel so stupid."

"Don't. There's no reason to." I wrap my arm over her shoulder and squeeze her in tight. She rests her head on my chest and I breathe in the smell of her hair. We stay there in silence for what seems like forever. I'm not sure what's going through her mind; I've never lived life as she has, as a defector. I can't help but think about the mark on her arm. *How was it possible for her to be at my school with a blue brand?*

As if reading my mind she says, "My parents work at the school. You've probably seen them around, tending the grounds. The educational board made a special exception for me to attend since the nearest defector school is so far away."

I try to think back to when I might have seen her parents at school but can't recall anything. As a senator's son, I rarely got the opportunity to meet the cleaning crew. Perhaps now that needed to change. "If they're half as nice as you, I can't wait to meet them."

Mary sat up and looked at me with her penetrating eyes. "Are you sure you're okay with this? It's against the law."

I shake my head. "Nowhere in the edict does it say that I can't date a defector. Only that we can't … well, you know."

Her cheeks blush and heat soon fills my face, too. The thought of us being intimate is something I know I'll one day crave but will never be allowed to act upon. I'm a true citizen of Primus. Mary is a defector. The law is clear that no risk of offspring can come from our union.

"It says fifth generation. Do you know why they defected?"

Mary shakes her head. "My grandfather never told me. I asked probably a hundred times before he was taken to the mines, but he'd always say the same thing, that the blue brand isn't what the senate tells everyone it is. My parents say the same thing."

"That's a funny thing to say. What is it, then?"

She shrugs. "I'm not really sure. Something about secrets and what really lies beyond the border wall, but we all know it's because my great-great-grandpa or someone else in my family tree wouldn't help fight in the atomic wars. Maybe it makes them feel better about it to make something up." She waves it off and we sit in silence, watching the sinking sun deepen the orange sky to red, turning the buildings into shadows.

I think back to the time I visited the coast before Mom died. The ocean was so beautiful, except for the tall cement pillars a few hundred yards from the beach that outlined the safety zone. Every now and then I'd see a ripple of electricity flow out from the pillars, revealing the electric fence that guards our borders. I remember one morning a deformed whale washed up on the sand, its body a mass of dying flesh. Dad warned me then about the poisons that hid beyond our border, and how I should never go near it. Maybe the blue brand was just a reminder to those that wore them of what really does lie beyond the safety zone; the sicknesses—the death. Without the blockade and barrier—our walls of Primus—protecting us, we would die like the rest of the planet.

I shake the morbid thoughts out of my head and scan the park for the ice cream vendor I saw a few minutes ago. I spot him laughing with a family near the entrance to the park. "How about we get some ice cream and end this date on a sweeter note?"

Mary laughs. "As long as they have chocolate, I'm game."

I take her hand in mine. She squeezes, and I squeeze back. She doesn't know it yet, but we are perfect together.

I WAKE. ALONE. I LIE IN THE NOW-FAMILIAR darkness until sleep takes me once more.

I DON'T KNOW HOW LONG I'VE BEEN CONFINED to solitary. There's no way of telling time, no way to know if I even still exist. I'm beginning to believe that I'm dead and this is hell. This is my punishment for a life not served in righteousness, a hell of my own making—my own eternal torment.

Sometimes I sing out into the lonely blackness, melodies Mom taught me as a child, hoping perhaps it will scare away the darkness. It doesn't. Sometimes I cry. Mostly I think; which is never good when I have nothing but regrets to think about. My body aches from lying on the hard floor. My only sustenance is the strangely sweet water in the toilet that I lap at like a dog. I wear nothing but the ratted underwear I was given at the beginning of the group battle, having removed the tunic to cover the smell of feces in the far corner of my cell by what I think is a drain. Perhaps this is what Katherine and her guards wanted. Perhaps this was the way humanity was stripped from a person, not through an identification number, but through lonely blackness.

Slim wouldn't want me getting out of shape, not after all the work he'd done. Even though it hurts, I exercise as much as I can. Part of me is surprised I even have the energy for it, but I do. I focus on pushups, sit-ups, and running in place. When I feel pain, I accept it and continue. It's my punishment after all—punishment for not being strong enough to protect Slim.

I can almost hear his voice inside my head, right next to my father's. Sometimes they argue with each other. Sometimes they argue with me, wanting me to explore this memory or that, both knowing that if I'd just think hard enough, I would discover the truth: who killed my father and why.

Sometimes I think about the exit sign I found in the tunnel. If only I'd had the strength to hold myself against the current, I could have unlatched the door and this blackness never would have happened. I think about that and do more pushups.

Part of me is grateful for the darkness of my cell. I think if I really saw what I look like, a stinking, starved, practically naked boy with a week or two's worth of stubble on his chin, I'd probably give up right here and now and let the Arena have me. In my mind, I remember who I was before I was branded CS4521. I am Calvin Thaddeus Sawyer, the son of the senate's consul. I am better than anything Katherine and her guards can throw at me. I will not become the number—I mustn't become the number.

"I'm still innocent!" I shout to the darkness. My voice echoes around the small cell, telling me how weak I sound. "I didn't kill my father, and you know it! You know it! I heard you say it yourself. Do you know who killed him? Do you? DO YOU?"

I wait, letting the words fade into nothing. There's no response, no audible proof that anything exists outside the walls of this cell.

I collapse to the cold floor and lean over the toilet. I splash cool water over my head until it drips down my neck and chest. It's not a person's touch but it's movement, and movement reminds me of life.

Katherine Marsh. Her name has to have a connection to my father. I remember when we first met and she spoke of him like she knew him. If so, I'd never heard him speak of her. Then again, I didn't want to know anything about the senate. Had I shown interest, I know Dad and Gerard would only have been on me more about making the senate my life's ambition. I saw what Dad had given up, an adoring wife, an eager son—I didn't want to do the same.

I think about the other fourteen senators, wondering if perhaps one of them is connected to the director, perhaps through family. Maybe one of the senators had a business dealing with the Arena, or maybe one in particular oversees the games themselves? The more I think, the more questions arise, questions without answers. You'd think for a guy at the top of his class, I'd be smarter. That must say loads about the quality of education in Primus.

My stomach practically roars with hunger as I feel the ache, the need, for something more than sweet water. I don't recall the last time I put food in my mouth. I'm not sure I can even recall the taste of it. I imagine sitting next to Slim at our table in the cafeteria, his plate laden high with every ounce of protein the Arena has to offer, and how he would lecture me on his first rule of survival: *food.* That if I was to think my way out of a situation I needed to feed my brain. How wise he seems right now.

"How are you enjoying your stay, CS4521?" Katherine's voice calls into my cell. In the darkness, the sound seems to come from every direction. I don't know how to respond. Part of me wonders if it's real. She sounds different from the voices of Dad or Slim that have been keeping me company. I wait, and her voice sounds again. "CS4521, I asked you a question."

If I tell her how I really feel, will she find pity in herself to free me, or will it only fuel her satisfaction in torturing me? I opt to say nothing.

"I have a treat for you," she says in an almost sing-song voice. "Your number has been announced for tonight's beast fight."

"My section won the group battle. That's not fair. I was awarded a break."

"You're an offender of the Arena," she shouts, hate filling her voice. "You do not have the right for a break. You fight when I tell you to fight."

"I won't fi—"

I hide my head in my hands as my cell fills with light and my eyes burn. It's so bright it feels as though I'm some mythical monster that will wither and turn to dust in the light. A slight vibration moves through the floor and suddenly the walls begin to sink. The floor is rising! I try to open my eyes to see what's going on, but it's too bright, and my eyes fill with tears.

A warm breeze blows down from above, and I welcome the freshness of it. I have been trapped with the odor of my cell so long I'd forgotten how clean air smells. The floor picks up momentum as it climbs higher and higher. I suddenly remember what Katherine said: a beast battle. *How can I fight in a beast battle?*

My stomach lurches with my body as the floor comes to a stop. I feel the dry, almost burning heat of the sun above me. The warm wind is so fast and dry it reminds me of the air driers in the showers down in the compound. Offenders do not have the right to towels. I stretch out my arms—the walls are gone. I crawl forward until my hand touches hot sand. *Am I in a desert? A beach?* I peer through the wind tearing at my eyes—*I need to see!*

An explosive, sizzling, buzz of a rattle sounds, almost coming from every direction. I tense, knowing what this sound belongs to. I wait for the strike to come.

-TWELVE-

I LEARNED ABOUT RATTLESNAKES YEARS AGO IN primary school. The snakes had fascinated me for years, from their forked tongue to the way they warn their victims before they strike. Our teacher had played a recording of their distinctive rattle and the sound had always made my skin crawl. But they, like most other animals in the wild, were supposed to have been wiped out by the atomic wars.

I don't move, hoping to show the snake I'm no threat. Again, I try to open my eyes to the blaring light around me, but a headache trumpets its way behind my skull, begging me to shut out the light. The rattle continues, filling my ears and tightening every last muscle in my body. I'm trying to determine which direction it's coming from—to the right, or maybe behind me. I shift to the left and a hiss accompanies the rattle. The snake is definitely behind me.

Not knowing what else to do, I ready myself for a blind sprint.

One. Two. Three.

I dash forward, expecting to feel the snap of the snake's

bite, but it doesn't connect. The spectators' roar fills the colosseum, giving me the strength to run. I don't care where I'm going, or that the hot sand is burning my soles; all I care is that I'm far away from that snake. When I can no longer hear the rattling, I stop, and once again focus on opening my eyes. I'm able to steal a peek here and there but I only get blurred images of light followed by a stabbing pain in my head. It's taking far too long for me to adjust to the light.

What a cruel trick for Katherine to play. Did she want me stumbling blind in the light only to die from a rattlesnake bite? The more I think of her, the more I hate her, the more I want to trade places with her and watch *her* die in the Arena.

"No!" I shout to myself. No matter the pain, no matter the hurt she causes me, I must hold onto who I am, Calvin Thaddeus Sawyer. I am not a number. I am not a killer.

I stand motionless for what seems a good three minutes before I open my eyes once more. When I do, I can finally see what nightmare the game masters have concocted for me.

The sky is a vibrant blue against deep gold sand that goes on forever. Heat ripples off the sand, making the landscape appear to move drunkenly about. In the far distance I see something—it's hard to make out, but it ripples in the haze, inviting me forward. Each step is agony now, making it harder to shut out the pain searing my feet.

What large beasts live in the desert? As hard as I think, the only large desert animal I can think of is a camel. I have a hard time seeing that as a threat. No, the game masters would want to make this beast fight entertaining. *Who wants to see a man fight a camel?*

Several species of snakes come to mind, including the rattlesnake and king cobra, but I still don't find snakes beastly enough for the game masters. Lizards, spiders, goats, and a few small wild cats are some of the animals I remember from my textbooks, but nothing large enough to kill a man without great effort. Then again, the game masters were never content on letting animals be what nature created them to be. Nature wasn't enough. They had to enhance them genetically, make them something new, something devious.

As I get closer to my target destination, I see what it is. I guess Katherine isn't denying me all the amenities the Arena has to offer. Sticking out of the sand is the halberd I used in my last two fights. Next to it is my kopis blade, some yellow fabric in a heap, sandals, and what appears to be a bag of food with a fat waterskin. I run to the objects with a surge of energy I haven't felt in days. Opening the bag of food, I find dried meat, nuts, and fruit, which I instantly begin to devour. They taste like a dream.

As I eat, I try to shield my skin from the sun's intense heat with the bundle of yellow fabric. I wrap some around my waist and more around my chest and shoulders. Remembering a story from my childhood about desert knights and magic carpets, I wrap the remaining fabric around my head, letting it drape down over my neck. The sandals are hot at first, having sat out in the sun, but they feel so much better than the sand once they're laced up past my ankles. I take one last bite of meat, drop the provisions bag onto my shoulder and pick up my weapons of war.

"Thank you, Bear," I say, aloud. These weapons have his name written all over them. Of course, I'd give credit for the food to Slim if he were alive. There's no way he'd have let me enter the Arena without a bag of food. The thought of his name fills my chest with pain and regret, but I can't afford to dwell on the dead. Not if I want to stay alive.

I'm sorry, Slim, I have to move on now.

Somewhat clothed and armed, I feel more capable of accepting the beast fight. Once again, I survey the terrain. To my displeasure, it hasn't changed. Nothing more than a wasteland of sand and heat. *How do I know which way to go?* If I choose the wrong direction, I could walk for miles and achieve nothing. No, the colosseum isn't miles long. I have to remember I'm in a building. I have an audience!

I hold the halberd high in the air. "Which way, people of Primus? Tell me which way to go!"

I drop the staff, pointing it toward the way I came. There is silence. I shift it and point it the opposite direction. Again silence. Perhaps they won't help me; perhaps they want me to wander aimlessly about until the heat of the desert takes me. I choose another direction and the audience approves my destination with a loud cry.

"Thank you, citizens of Primus!"

The cheers grow louder, and I can't help but smile. This

is what my father must have felt as he stood before crowds. I lift the halberd high into the air and scream a war cry as I charge forward. "For Primus! For my father!"

Triumphant cheers fill my ears as I run through the sand. I'm not prepared to kill, I'm not sure I'm capable of it, but if it comes to a fight to the death against me and a creature bred in a test tube, I will be the victor. I will be the one the crowds of Primus cheer for.

Sand sticks to my sweaty legs as I continue onward through the rippling heat. I wonder how long I will have to run before I meet my foe. The audience continues to cheer me on, but with no destination in sight, I fear running out of momentum before I come close to confronting my fate.

Then I see something, something that brings me to a sudden stop. The sand is moving—rolling!

I tighten the grip on my staff and search my mind, desperate to recall anything from my studies that would involve a creature that could move sand like that. Whatever lies beneath the sand has to be a monster, something huge. I think of dinosaurs and work my mind forward, mentally rushing through the index of animals that used to live on this planet. I shake my head. I've seen the game masters use mythical creatures, too. I recall two instances where an offender fought a Minotaur in a maze, and another offender fought a type of dragon in a castle. Both were creations of the Arena, both fictional beasts brought to life. Perhaps this is yet another test tube experiment, some type of sand dweller.

There was one legend—a creature that lived in the sands of what used to be Mongolia. They called it a death worm.

I tense as the sand beneath me lifts, then settles down. Before me, the sand churns as if a great plug has been pulled and the sand is draining away. The sand shifts, and a creature bursts out. I gasp along with the audience as the vile monstrosity shows its ugly form. Most of its body is hidden beneath the sand but what surfaces is as wide as a bus with pink skin and bristling, barbed hair.

A toxic smell forces me back as the death worm spreads its wide pincer mouth and ejects thick goo that sizzles as it hits the sand at my feet. Instinct tells me the goo is something I don't want to touch. The death worm gurgles a roar as it plunges its fat, segmented body back into the sand. Again the ground beneath me shifts, and I know it's only a matter a minutes before the thing swallows me whole. Even in my wildest nightmares, this was not how I imagined I'd die.

The ground pushes up, reaches for me. I leap to the side and roll down the rising mound. The death worm bursts out of the sand with a wild growl. Sand sizzles around me as more of the tar-like substance explodes out of the beast's gaping mouth. Instantly the death worm buries itself in the sand and I feel it moving beneath me again.

I scramble back, sliding downward. My momentum causes me to flip over and the halberd flies from my grip as I roll to a stop. The death worm surges out of the sand exactly where I stood moments before. It moves its head around, trying to find me, its barbed hair searching like tentacles. I can't see any eyes, but the creature locates me in an instant. Its large mouth shrinks then expands, spitting the dark, toxic goo toward me. I jump back, but some of the poison slaps against my leg. Searing pain shoots up my calf and into my thigh and I'm thrown onto my rear. Though I try to appear strong, a scream bursts from my mouth. The worm spits again, this time narrowly missing my torso. I crawl backward, my elbows digging into the hot sand.

I need distance.

The halberd glints in the sunlight a few feet away. I need the staff if I'm to survive this monster. I tear the fabric from my head and use it to wipe away the black goo on my leg. Blood and tissue come away with it. I don't have time to deal with the pain; I have to ignore it, to push on. The death worm dives back into the sand.

Digging deep for the last of my energy reserves, I get to my feet and run toward the halberd. In seconds I have the staff in hand. I run away from the pit the death worm created and turn around. The sand rolls toward me, and I flip the halberd over, blade down. The crowd shouts out warnings as the hill begins to rise. I wait. Every second crawls by as if in slow motion. *This is it!*

One. Two.

Three.

I slam the halberd's blade as hard as I can into the sand. It's met with a rumble and abruptly I'm airborne. I crash down into the sand ten feet away from where I started, flipping over a few times before I come to a stop. The cheering crowd almost drowns out the raging death worm's cry as it whips its head back and forth, the halberd firmly planted in the flesh of its mouth.

I can't believe my idea actually worked. I didn't kill it, but I did wound it. The worm continues to shake, flinging itself from side to side. Finally it frees the staff from its mouth, sending it flying. The barbed hairs search the sand and I wonder if the creature's blind and uses touch to see, or maybe it senses the vibrations in the ground. I try my best to hold perfectly still.

Deciding to test my theory, I slowly pull a handful of nuts from my bag. I bite my lower lip, knowing Slim would be rolling in his grave to see me wasting food. I toss the nuts as far to the left of the creature as I can. They thump to the sand and I see the barbed hairs ripple across the death worm's skin. In an instant it's back in the ground, heading toward the nuts. I toss a few more and watch from a safe distance.

This time the worm doesn't build a mound, but circles the nuts round and round. I toss another nut, trying to coax it out, but oddly, it continues to circle. The ground vibrates and suddenly the nuts, and the sand beneath them, are swallowed up by a sinkhole. Dust flies out from the hole as the worm attacks the nuts. I cringe, knowing now every step I take tells this creature where I am. And worse: it attacks differently each time.

I search the sand for the halberd and find it a few yards away. Reaching back into my bag, I grab the remaining nuts. I need to create a distraction that will give me enough time to cross the distance between myself and my weapon. I toss the nuts as hard as I can in the opposite direction. Sand rolls toward them. I wait a beat, then run as fast as I can toward the halberd. The death worm instantly changes course.

Two yards.

One.

The worm erupts from the sand, its long, fat body wriggling forward. I skid to a stop, ducking as it snaps its pincer mouth just above my head. I pull the kopis from my waistband and slash my arm in an arc, just the way Hammer showed me. The blade drags along the worm's skin, slicing a deep ravine as it goes.

The creature howls in pain and the crowd cheers. The beast writhes backward, and I use the moment to escape its reach.

I find the halberd and waste no time stabbing the side of the death worm. It howls again, and again, I stab it. The crowd is in hysterics now, filling the colosseum with a roar that vibrates the sand. Propelled by their enthusiasm, I stab the creature once more, then hold the halberd up like an emblem of power. I search the blue sky, wishing for once I could see the faces of the people. Their cheers rocket through me and I'm filled with glory.

Then, there is silence.

I turn back to the death worm and find nothing but sand. I wounded it, but the beast isn't dead. The fight is not over.

-THIRTEEN-

I WAIT BENEATH THE HOT SUN FOR WHAT FEELS like hours. The death worm is either dead or has given up. I wonder what the game masters do if a beast simply doesn't want to fight. Do they prod it along, perhaps deny it food, or maybe offer a tantalizing reward? Offenders don't have the option to give up; to give up means to accept death. I imagine the spectators are growing bored with the fall in action, so the game masters will need do something soon.

I use the time to clean the wound on my leg with the waterskin. Whatever the death worm's goo contains, it removed a few layers of skin. The wound hurts as I bandage it, but I can't waste effort dwelling on the pain. I eat the remaining food in my bag and down the rest of my water. Hopefully, the beast battle will end before I die of dehydration.

"Come on with it!" I shout to the sky. "Don't leave these people waiting."

Applause fills the colosseum, but minutes later I'm still waiting, baking in the torturous heat. I search the landscape, looking for the death worm—or anything else that might move in this arid world. I try pointing the halberd in all directions in hopes the spectators will disclose the location of the creature, but they remain silent. Do they know where the worm is and they're just not telling me? Perhaps they don't know, or maybe the game masters have prohibited them from giving me clues.

The sun begins to lower in the illusion of the sky and it makes me wonder if the death worm is really a nocturnal beast. Perhaps this is the game masters' way of coaxing it out of hiding. In nature, the sun would never set so fast. When the sky reaches a deep red, I lift my halberd once more, and hope I'm wrong about the game masters interfering with the crowd.

The audience cheers.

This is it. I point the halberd in three directions before they boom a positive response. I give a nod of appreciation and run toward my target.

The ground beneath me gives way.

My back slaps against clammy clay ground and the air rushes from my lungs. Sand and dust block out what remains of the blood-red sky. When I start to get my bearings, I find I'm in a circular pit that has to be at least fifty yards wide. All around me, wide tunnels lead in all directions under the desert sand. This is not good. Not good at all.

With my chest aching, I roll to my side and push off the ground. I grab the halberd and slowly take in what I pray will not be my grave. There's no sign of the death worm, but I know the beast created this pit. It will come for me soon.

Movement on the wall of dirt and sand catches my eye and, despite the heat, a chill runs up my back. The fallout must have disturbed a rattlesnake's den. The snake tries to climb up the wall but loses its hold and flops to the ground. The den breaks apart and three smaller snakes drop, landing next to their mother. My heart races. I know that rattlesnakes can be deadly, but most adult snakes don't release all their venom in one bite. Young rattlesnakes can take down large animals with one bite. Unlike their mother, these young snakes won't give any warning before they strike.

I search the walls, trying to find the best way to climb out of this pit of death. One section of the wall looks promising, but proves worthless. The wall is so fragile that sand and dirt just pull away with my slightest touch. The only way out seem to be the various tunnels that lead off to who-knows-where. The snakes begin to slither closer, but they keep to the perimeter of the pit. I move to the center to avoid contact with them.

The ground shudders and the pit fills with the sizzling buzz of the mother snake's rattle. I tense, and lean on the halberd for support.

Dirt and sand balloon toward at me as the death worm squirms its way into the pit from one of the tunnels. The barbed hairs on its pink skin feel about, searching, seeking. It shifts its head, focusing on the vibrations of the mother snake's rattle, and spits a glob of black goo directly at her. The young snakes hiss as the thick goo dissolves their mother until there's nothing left.

As slowly and carefully as I can, I pull my provisions bag off my shoulder. Hopefully, I can fool the worm into looking the other way again. I swing my arm back and let the bag go. It smacks against the opposite wall, dislodging sand and dirt before it thumps to the ground. The death worm shifts its ugly head, and I charge.

It swings its head toward me. Its mouth shrinks and expands, but before it can spit its goo, I launch my halberd. The sharp blade slides into the death worm's mouth with a sickening squish. The beast, along with the crowd of spectators, fills the pit with a deafening roar. The death worm writhes and wriggles, trying to free the staff. I pull the kopis from my waistband and begin slashing its hide. The skin around its mouth is too thick. I might as well be trying to carve up a slab of granite. I do manage to remove several barbed hairs, hopefully blinding the monster.

Its back end slaps against the pit wall, causing sand and dirt to crash down on me. In a panic, I try to climb out of the debris, but find the sand swallowing up my legs. I drop the kopis in my efforts to escape, and the sand is up to my chest before the landslide stops. The death worm continues to thrash about, the halberd sunk deeply in its mouth. It moans pathetically and I can't help but feel sick, knowing I'm the one who forced those sounds. I'm not sure how many more times I can strike out at the creature. It's ugly and it wants to kill me, but with every blow, every cry, I feel I am turning into a monster myself. I don't want to be a killer.

I climb atop the mound that half-buried me and slowly climb out of the pit. The kopis is lost to the sand below, and the halberd irretrievable. If the Arena sends anymore creatures after me, I'll be defenseless.

The death worm's scream changes, filling my ears with a sound that's almost too much to bear. As if led by a mad conductor, the spectators in the colosseum cheer. It's a cacophony of triumph and pain.

The death worm twists, trembles, then slaps to the clay floor. I'm confused how the halberd killed the worm, when it only seemed to injure it—until I see the three young rattlesnakes slide over the worm's body. I let out a sigh as I rest my hands on my knees. The fight is over.

A trumpet blares and a beam of light shoots down from the dark sky, resting on a platform a few yards away. I slowly stagger toward it.

I'm just steps away when it dawns on me that I need to thank the spectators. Without them I wouldn't have gotten as far as I did. I lift my hands high in the air. "Thank you, people of Primus! The victory is yours!"

Cheers and shouts of praise fill my ears as I step onto the platform and it lowers me beneath the Arena.

I continue to look up as the light dims and the sound of the spectators fades away. Soon I'm at the bottom of the shaft, looking at the conveyer that leads back into the compound. I'm grateful Katherine has decided my time in solitary confinement is over. I long for three things: food, a hot shower, and my bed. They're not much, but after having my rights to them revoked for so long, they seem like everything.

When I enter the mirrored room, I'm met by a circle of thin, disheveled young men in stained yellow wrappings. I reach out my hand in a greeting and discover it's my reflection. I can't believe how different I look. Dark hair covers my chin in patches and my eyes are hollow spheres. I no longer resemble the boy that entered the Arena those few weeks ago. Katherine has done a great job of stripping me of my humanity, but she hasn't won yet. I might not look the same, but I know who I am. And I know I don't belong here.

The mirror in the back of the room slides open and Bear enters. His brown face is stoic as usual, but I welcome it with a smile. Without thinking, I rush over to him and throw an arm around his neck. I expect him to pull away or knock me to the floor, but he doesn't. Instead he wraps his thick arms around me and gives me the biggest bear hug of all time.

It's touch! Wonderful, living, breathing, touch!

"You did good, Kid. You did good."

I want to tell him how hard it was—lying day after day in the dark of that hopeless prison. I want to complain about how humiliating it was for me to drink from a toilet and piss in the corner. I want to tell him how much it hurts inside to know that I got Slim killed. But the longer Bear holds me, the more it doesn't matter. For so long I had to be strong to survive in this hell, but for this moment Bear's friendship allows me to show emotion. For the first time in a really long time, I feel like someone cares for me, cares enough to hold me. He doesn't pull away. He doesn't call me a sissy. He holds me like a father holds a son. I can't help but think how I wished my own father would have held me this way.

"Thanks for the halberd." I pull away and wipe at my face.

"You used it well."

"And the food—I haven't eaten in such a long time. Thanks for that, too."

Bear grunts. "The food was Slim's idea. Something about *fueling your stomach to think better.* That man has his anatomy screwed up if you ask me."

My heart literally skips a beat. *Did he say Slim?*

Before I can ask, a pounding sounds on the door to the armory. I can hear shouting. Bear's stoic face betrays a wide smile. "Someone's a little anxious to see you, Kid. You better go open that door before he busts his fat butt through it."

I don't hesitate. I charge through the armory and slam my hand against the panel, unlocking the door. It opens and I'm once again caught in a life-giving embrace.

-FOURTEEN-

I SPEND ALMOST HALF AN HOUR LETTING THE hot water shower away the memories of the past weeks. Despite my sunburned skin, it feels wonderful to wash away the dirt and human stink. Slim shouts for me to be done, and I turn off the faucet and quickly dry under the blowers before pulling on the gray pants of an offender. I take my time shaving though, having never had so much hair to remove from my face before. The electric razor clogs three times before I'm finished and I've managed to nick my skin five times.

Slim laughs. "Man, Kid, did your daddy never teach you to shave?"

I shrug. He taught me two years ago when I barely had peach fuzz on my chin. Only then I had a top of the line electric razor and never worried about it slicing my skin open.

"Forget it," Slim says, tossing me a shirt. "Let's go eat."

The thought of food makes my stomach rumble. I feel as though I could eat an entire cow.

"Don't eat too fast," Slim instructs as we head down the glass hallway. "Your stomach has shrunk. You want to stretch it slowly."

"Giving the kid tips on how to get a gut as big as yours?" Hammer asks, shoving a playful elbow into Slim's stomach. He walks without a limp, so I assume his leg has healed. "It's good to have you back, Kid." He slaps me on the back before racing ahead of us, stopping only a second to wave up to one of the cameras pointed down our hall.

I stop. Slim takes a few steps, then turns around. "What's wrong?"

"How long was I gone?"

Slim's eyebrows lift, creasing his forehead. "You've been in solitary for fifteen days."

"Fifteen? How am I still alive?"

Slim puts his arm around me and gently pulls me toward the cafeteria. "I've heard a man can go three to four weeks without food if he has water. Bear lasted twelve days when they threw *him* in solitary."

"Bear was in solitary?"

"Oh yeah. This was a while back. From what I hear, you and Bear are the only ones they bothered trying to shut up."

"Why was Bear in solitary?"

Slim leaned his head close to mine and whispered, "He won't talk about it. I hear his number was called one night, but he didn't show up. Then when they finally got him in the Arena, he refused to fight. They say he knelt down and exposed his neck for the guy to kill him."

"How did he—"

"Survive?" Slim laughed. "Kid, when you're in the Arena, you have to play by their rules. It's against the rules to willingly die. The game masters shot the other offender in the back of the head and then they threw Bear in the clink. When he came out, he refused to go by his number anymore and got pretty angry with those that ever dared call him it. Even now, when he has to fight, they call him Bear. He's the only one they do that for. It's like that solitary earned him respect from the legs up in the control room."

"You mean Katherine Marsh?"

"Is that her name?" Slim asked with a smile. "Kid, you know everyone, don't you? Let me guess: your daddy used to have her over for Sunday brunch with the other senators."

"Not that I know. But she knows I didn't kill him. She said so herself."

"And look how she shows her support of the truth, right?"

We enter the cafeteria and the room falls quiet. The men look up, eyes following me, as Slim and I make our way to the food counter. I see Slaughter and the other cronies in Section Six huddled in the back corner. He has a wicked smile on his scarred face. I quickly look away—there are other people I'd rather see than Slaughter's ugly mug.

"Alright, people, why don't you take a picture?" Slim says. "What, you never seen a person survive a beast fight after two weeks in solitary?"

The offenders return to their food and pick up their abandoned conversations. I grab a plate and begin loading it with food. After taking a cup of water, I follow Slim to our normal spot under the big monitors.

Two familiar faces fill the screen, and I'm shocked by the caption underneath: *Senators Jacob Billings and Norma Watson murdered. No suspect in custody.*

"What? When did this—"

Slim shushes me and nods toward the screen.

"Authorities are perplexed by this latest crime streak targeting senate members," the news anchor says. "People fear that Senators Billings and Watson are just the beginning and security has been heightened to protect our nation's leaders. Many are blaming the defectors for these murders. The leader of the defectors, however, claims they had nothing to do with it."

The screen switches to a group of protesters outside Senate Hall. A man stands at the podium, trying his best to quiet an angry crowd. It takes me a moment to recognize him—it's Mary's father. "We have done our best to try to solve our differences without violence. If the murder of these senators was committed by a citizen you label as a defector, this person is not associated with our party. We seek nothing more than the rights and privileges of all the inhabitants of Primus. We seek this peacefully."

"Liars!" a woman shouts. Several people charge the podium, and armed guards struggle to push the crowd back. The view returns to the news anchor.

"Malcolm Omphrey was taken into custody shortly after his speech. Although he has not been officially arrested for any crimes, many believe him to be the mastermind behind the spree of defector violence against the senate. Senator Lindt reminds the public that this is just a precaution and asks for us not to jump to conclusions."

"That's a load of crap!" I shout. "Mary's dad isn't a mastermind killing senators!"

"Settle down, Kid," Slim warns.

I turn to him and struggle to keep my voice to a whisper. "This has to do with my father's murder, I know it!"

"Don't go jumping the gun."

"Slim, those senators were at my house the night my father died. I saw them!"

Slim puts up a hand to silence me.

"Not here," he whispers.

Suddenly I'm aware of the eyes and cameras in the room. I look up and see myself on the monitor. It's a shot of me right after winning the group battle. I stand in a muddy field shouting up at the sky. *"I want out! I'm innocent! I didn't kill my father!"*

"Authorities are still trying to dispel the surprising declaration of innocence as seen two weeks ago, following a victory in the Arena. Offender CS4521, previously known as Calvin Sawyer, the son of the late Senator Thaddeus Sawyer, declared that he did not, in fact, kill his father. Some are calling for a full investigation into these assertions; others are seeing this as a madman's cry for attention."

The scene shows a shot from a hovercam inside one of the hallways in Senate Hall. Senator Gerard rushes down the hall. "Please, Senator, can you give us your insight on Calvin Sawyer's declaration?"

"I've already given my opinion on the matter. If you'll excuse me." I can't help but smile at Gerard. He reminds me of Dad, never wanting to repeat the same thing twice.

"But sir, he's saying he's innocent. Didn't you once say the boy was like a nephew to you?"

Gerard stops and looks directly into the camera. "We all know Calvin is guilty. It's true I once cared for him, but I believe this is an outcry from a spoiled, mentally-unwell boy that wants his charmed life back. He killed his father. End of discussion."

My heart sinks. How could he say that about me? I loved Gerard. He'd been there for me when Mom died; he talked with me when Dad ignored me. How could he say that about me? Couldn't he see that I didn't do it?

"Offender CS4521 may have been sent to the Arena for murder, but perhaps we should now add theft to his list of crimes. He has surely stolen the eyes of many in Primus," the news anchor says. The screen shows me during the last battle holding up the halberd to the crowd.

"Which way, people of Primus? Tell me which way to go!"

Now I'm fighting the death worm. I see the crowd in the stadium seating, some watching the scene below, others fixated on the enormous screens displaying a close up of my sweaty, sunburned body. People are on their feet, shouting and cheering as if I'm a hero. A hovercam zooms in on a group of teenage girls.

"What do you think about offender CS4521?" the news anchor asks through the hovercam.

"Oh, he's dreamy!" one girl says. She giggles, and the rest of the girls laugh with her.

The screen returns to the news anchor. Behind him is a picture of me frozen in midair, holding the halberd in one hand, the kopis in the other. The brilliant sun gleams on my nearly-naked body, dramatically enhancing my newly acquired muscles. I don't understand how they're turning me into some heroic icon, an idol for teenage girls to fantasize over. That picture makes me look like an offender—like a killer.

No! I don't want to look that way! I push off from the table and charge out of the cafeteria. My feet slap against the cold floor as I head down Section One's hallway. I move past the dormitories and into the rec room. In a few minutes, I'm at the top of the climbing wall. I lie back and try to shut out the sound of the news monitor above the bleachers recapping my fight with the death worm. I wish it would all just go away.

"I have to say, Kid, that was the fastest I've ever seen you climb this wall." Slim pulls his large body onto the platform and slaps my leg. "You okay?"

I don't answer. Of course I'm not okay. My father's best friend, who is supposed to support me, just told the world I'm a killer. Then the Arena proved it by showing them how ruthless I am. What hope do I have of getting out of this hell? No, I'm not okay.

"I can't stay here anymore, Slim. I can't. I don't want to kill."

"I know," he whispers. "I know. And I've found a way out."

I sit up. "What?"

Slim looks around the rec room, checking for listeners. Finally content, he pulls in so close I can smell the fried chicken on his breath. "The past two weeks, me and Bear have been busy. I think we've come up with a way … to escape."

-FIFTEEN-

I FOLLOW SLIM AND SOME OF THE OTHER members of Section One as we file onto a conveyer that will take us under the Arena. Most of the men in our section were assigned farming, kitchen, or laundry duties. Slim, Bear, and the other men, including me, have been assigned building maintenance. I'm not sure what it all entails, but according to Slim, it means we're responsible for caring for the underbelly of the colosseum.

The conveyer pulls us through a cement tunnel lit every few yards with a dim bulb. The trip seems to take forever, and I wonder again how far the compound is from the actual Arena. I remember a few overhead shots from past episodes of the fights but don't recall ever seeing the compound, only the massive oval structure of the colosseum with its high arches and sculpted statues of gods from long ago. Perhaps the compound is completely hidden underground, or maybe we are just so far away, I never saw the building in the footage. The vastness of our prison only makes the thought of escaping even more impossible.

The offenders in front of me speak to each other in whispers. I catch little jokes here and there, most of them perverted or political jabs at the senate. I don't engage. Slim is as silent as Bear, and I am silent, watching them. I don't understand, and part of that concerns me.

Soon the tunnel opens up into a large area. Thick steel columns reach up to a high ceiling that is separated in a grid with several trapdoors, all with numbers painted on them. Gigantic pillars reach up to the ceiling, surrounded by metal catwalks, large tubes and pipes that run along the top. I turn to Slim and whisper, "Is the Arena up above?"

He nods, but says nothing as the conveyer comes to a stop.

"You all know your sectors," Bear calls out. "Kid, you can come with me and Slim to inspect sectors sixteen through thirty-two."

"We inspected those sectors a week ago," a stout man says. He has flaming red hair and a tattoo of a spider's web lacing down his neck. "You don't have to do them again."

Bear narrows his dark eyes. "Last time I checked, the control room left me in charge." As if to reiterate his authority, he taps the small tablet in his hands with his index finger. I wonder if each sector has a leader like Bear that Katherine gives orders through. "It says right here that sectors sixteen through thirty-two need rechecking. Maybe you didn't do your job when you were there?"

"Don't tell me I didn't do my job! I did just what I was

told to do. I didn't find any issues with the pipes, plumbing, or doors. Maybe it's you that messed up the report."

"I don't make mistakes." Bear stands straighter, and the redhead backs away. I don't blame him—Bear is at least twice as big as he is. "Kid. Slim. Follow me."

I glance over to the long wall and see each sector number clearly written out in bold black lettering. It starts at three hundred and goes down from there. Each sector is about four yards wide. I do the math in my head and try not to groan. This is going to be a long walk.

The area is so vast I can't see the opposite wall. I turn to Slim and whisper, "How big is this place?"

"Do I look like a freakin' architect? It's big. That's all I know. See those big tubes? The really fat, black ones?" He points up at the ceiling. "Those are the conveyers that take you to the lifts."

As we walk, I try to map out the colosseum in my mind. If the pipes are the conveyers that lead to the lifts, we still have to be hundreds of feet below the actual fighting ground. So much effort had to go into designing this massive structure. And all of it just to watch men die.

The other offenders climb ladders up to catwalks. While we walk, I watch them each pick up a bag of tools hanging from a line of hooks mounted to the cement walls as they go. Both Bear and Slim grab the last remaining bags and hoist them over their shoulders.

"We'll find an extra one along the way," Slim says.

"You'd think they'd offer carts or something. It sure would make the work go faster."

Slim gives a fake laugh. "Man, oh man, Kid, you think they care if the work goes fast or not? This is slave labor. I think they get all warm and fuzzy inside the harder they make it for us."

"I always imagined that the Arena had a bunch of employees doing all this. Don't they have engineers or something?"

"Sure they do. They send them in to repair things we can't—but why pay an engineer to come fix a leaky pipe when you can pay us nothing? The whole thing is self-operational. We clean it, fix it, even feed the monsters they cook up in the labs once they're put into the cages. It's kind of funny when you think about it. We basically help kill ourselves."

"We feed the monsters?"

Slim laughs again. "Yeah. We didn't get assigned in this rotation, but sooner or later they'll come up again. You really don't want that assignment, anyway. Some guys are stupid and don't follow the rules, then they really do feed them … if you catch my drift."

Bear turns around to shoot Slim an irritated glare.

"What? The kid's going to learn one day or another. This place isn't all chocolates and roses."

We pass by sector one hundred fifty and I notice large wooden crates lining the wall. They stand about five feet tall and nine feet long. "What's in the crates?"

“Don’t know. Don’t care,” Slim says, stepping around the large wooden boxes.

I can’t help but wonder what’s inside. Each crate is marked with the logo of the Arena on its side. As we pass, I inspect the backside of the crates, expecting some type of clue to reveal its contents. I see nothing, but run into the back of Bear. It feels like running into a wall. The man doesn’t even move. Like Slim, he just stands there, frozen. I follow their gaze, and I understand why.

A dozen ancient-style warships line the walls. They rest on great wooden frames and look like they were pulled straight from an ancient world history textbook—the world before the atomic wars. They’re beautiful, with red-brown wood and gleaming metal. One ship has twenty-five port holes along its side, like twenty-five eyes glaring at us. Each ship is garishly marked with the brightly-colored logo of Gerard Electronics. I’m pretty sure that’s not historically accurate. Obviously Senator Gerard was the sponsor of whatever these ships will be used for. I doubt their appearance in the Arena will offer enough commercial return to pay for their construction. Maybe Senator Gerard just really wants to see a naval battle played out in the Arena. Gerard was always fascinated with pre-atomic wars history. He had a thing for the American Revolution and the American Civil War and collected any bits of memorabilia he could find, wasting no expense. We even built a few model ships like these together, although they never looked as good.

It really was his obsession for history that encouraged me to love it too.

"They're called galleys," I say, eager to show off what I learned about ancient naval battles from Gerard. "They used them to fight wars on water. The portholes on the sides are for the oars."

"Man-powered ships?" Slim mumbles. "Look at all the ships. That's a lot of man power. What the hell are those game masters up to?"

"Shut it!" Bear hisses.

The sound of several pairs of boots pounding the cement floor reaches my ears. My heart races. Should we be here? What will happen to us if they find us down here? Bear takes a few steps backward, and Slim and I do the same.

A line of six guards in crimson uniforms steps out from the back of the furthest galley. Today they don't wear their masks, and I can see them for what they truly are: men—human men. I'd imagined them as robots or hybrid concoctions brewed in the labs. But they're definitely human. Some even wear pleasant smiles, as if enjoying their day. Until they notice us.

"Stop!" someone orders. Were they telling us not to run, or not to come any closer? A few of the men pull batons from their belts, which they hold close to their chests.

"This is a restricted area," the leader of them says.

"We have authorization," Bear replies coolly.

"Offenders are not authorized anything." The chisel-jawed, blond officer scowls at Bear. He slowly withdraws his baton from his belt and tightens his fist around it, a slight smile lifting the corner of his mouth. He looks like he enjoys hurting others. Maybe it's a requirement for working here.

Bear holds up his hands, his tablet in one of them. "We don't want any trouble. We have orders to check sectors sixteen through thirty—"

"No talking!" the officer shouts, taking a few steps forward. "Those sectors have already been signed off. You are out of bounds."

The guards stand at the ready, as still and emotionless as robots. Their eyes are dark and full of hate and I realize they don't see us as humans, either. They only see criminals to be punished; criminals with no human rights.

"Please, check your reports before this goes any further," Bear pleads. "I don't want any—"

"I said, no talking!" An officer charges toward us with his baton held high. The five guards behind him watch, each with their teeth gritted together in a savage growl. Bear gives a slight shake of his head as if warning me and Slim to step back. He drops the tablet. It crashes to the floor seconds before the baton is swung at his head.

Bear grabs the man's wrist, gives it a violent shake, and the baton clatters to the floor. He spins the guard around, wrapping his arm about the officer's head with his other hand braced on the side of it. In an instant, he could snap the man's neck. The other guards' faces turn to shock. They underestimated Bear, a man who has survived for years by killing others with his bare hands.

"Check your shankin' report. NOW!"

One guard pulls a tablet from a bag strapped over his shoulder and nervously taps at its screen. I don't dare breathe, let alone move. I know that Bear has killed before, otherwise he wouldn't still be here, but I don't want to see him actually do it. I fear if I see him kill, he will always be a killer to me. Right now he's a friend, and I want him to stay that way.

Slim looks like he's on the verge of throwing up. I haven't seen him look this way since our encounter with Slaughter in the cafeteria. Now I'm not sure which he fears more, the guards or Slaughter. It could be a toss-up.

The seconds drag by like minutes. Bear doesn't budge a muscle, and the officer pants so loud he sounds like a rabid dog. I check his mouth to make sure he's not foaming.

The guard with the tablet looks up. "He's right. They were notified this morning to recheck the plumbing and duct work for a possible contamination leak in the area."

Bear lets go, and the officer drops to the floor. "I need a new tablet to file my report." Bear reaches out to the man with the tablet.

"I can't … this is mine."

"Damn it, Dixon! Give him the tablet!" his leader orders, getting up off the floor. He rubs his neck and stoops down to pick up his baton. He backs to his men, never once taking his eyes off Bear.

Dixon hesitates, then hands Bear the tablet.

"This was all a misunderstanding," the officer says. "Dixon, pick up the broken tablet that *you* dropped."

Dixon turns around, shooting his commander a quizzical look.

"Do it!" his leader orders.

Now red-faced, Dixon bends down and picks up the shattered tablet. No doubt he'll be reprimanded for breaking the Arena's equipment. He returns to the line of men and slips the damaged device into his bag.

The officer eyes us with a dark look, his brow cemented in a scowl. "It's best if everyone forgets what just happened. That way nobody gets hurt."

Bear remains perfectly still as the guards file out and the door slams shut behind them. It's only then that I breathe normally again. Slim lets out an exasperated sigh and wipes the sweat from his forehead.

"That was freakin' insane!"

"Let's move," Bear says. He marches forward as if the encounter with the guards never happened. Perhaps he's doing just what the leader said, forgetting the whole thing. But as Bear holds the new tablet ever closer to his side, I know there's more to what just happened.

-SIXTEEN-

THE VIEW FROM THE CATWALK IS DIZZYING. Heights normally don't bother me, but standing hundreds of feet in the air with only a narrow, grated metal walkway beneath one's feet can change one's perspective. I try not to think about crashing onto the cement floor and instead focus on my task, which is inspecting the giant black tube that stretches from one wall to the other. The light from the little flashlight I found in the tool bag only proves that the Arena is clean and well-maintained. I can't find a single trace of a spider's web, dust bunny, or leaky pipe.

Seeing nothing more to check, I move on to the next row of pipe work, resting for a moment on the cement pad that connects each walkway. The grates in the floor hurt my feet. I'm sure the engineer who designed this particular feature of the building didn't know barefooted men would be the ones using it. I give myself a minute more, then head to the next row.

I crane my neck downward, trying to find Slim and Bear. They went ahead after showing me what to do. They planned to work their way back to me, but I haven't heard them for some time. I thought we should have met up by now since I've already inspected eleven rows. My hope is to find their feet resting on the catwalks but I see nothing but rows of metal and pipes—and the twelve war ships in the distance.

"Shankin' idiot!" I scold myself.

I return to the platform and check the wall for the sector number. The number forty-seven stares back at me like some billboard announcing my stupidity. For the past few hours I've been inspecting the wrong freaking rows! I should have gone left and continued left, instead I went right. *Proud moment for me, Dad. Make sure the hovercam takes a good picture.*

I drop my tool bag to the platform and take a moment to relax my feet before having to walk all the way back to sector thirty-six and begin working in the right direction. I slouch against the cement wall and welcome its cool touch against my back. The soft hum of the pipes begs me to close my eyes, and I willingly obey. The sound of the hum grows louder as I listen, as if they're filling with water. The idea of water reminds me of the electric green sign that read *Emergency Exit.*

I sit up and look down the length of wall toward the war ships. Three sectors of catwalks away, I see it. The number fifty stamped out on the wall in blue paint. I get to my feet and hurry along the length of the catwalk, passing each sector without a glance. When I get to sector fifty, I begin examining the pipe work.

Nothing about this sector seems any different than the rest. I shine the flashlight around the fat tubes and pipes expecting to see a much larger pipe that would carry water, but I don't see anything unusual. When I finally reach the opposite wall, I'm greeted by nothing but cement. Disappointed, I shake my head for wasting even more time. I'm about to leave when something farther down the catwalk catches my eye—a metal ladder that climbs up the wall from the catwalk into an opening big enough for a man. This is the something different I was looking for. My heart pounds with the possibilities.

I rush over to the ladder and check in both directions before climbing up. One rung after the next, I move into the narrow tunnel and continue upward. After I've climbed for several minutes, I look down and see a small circle of light leading back to the catwalk. I must have climbed at least fifty feet. I reach into the bag and pull out the flashlight, shining it up toward the emptiness above me. The ladder seems to go on forever. I hesitate going any further. If I don't meet up with Slim and Bear soon, I might miss the conveyer back into the compound. The last thing I need is those guards to come looking for me. Then again, if this ladder leads to what I think it does, it might help in our escape.

Escape … Do I really think this ladder will lead me to a magical door that will get me out of this building? Yes and no. In the Arena nothing is for sure. But if I don't check what it is, I'll always wonder if this was my way out and I didn't ever take it. The idea of finding out exactly what it is gives me the strength to climb higher.

I continue climbing until I'm forced to take another break because my legs and arms are throbbing. The light below is no wider than a coin. I reach for the flashlight again and press it on, shining it above me. I smile when I see that, just a few feet higher, there's a platform, and next to it, a large hatch with a rotary wheel. I race up the ladder and fall onto the wheel. It sticks for a moment, then spins easily around.

The hatch opens and the dim green glow of the emergency exit sign glints on the damp surface inside the tunnel. There might not be a rushing river of water, but I'm certain this is the tunnel I was fed through during the group battle. If I were to go in, it would take me to the fighting ground.

With a mad grin, I close the hatch and inspect the rest of the platform. A set of metal steps leads up to a locked door with an electronic keypad next to it. I recall all the locked doors I passed just to get into the compound. Behind this locked door is probably another locked door, and probably another one after that. I'm beginning to think climbing the ladder was just another indication of how stupid I am.

I readjust the bag over my shoulder and start down the rungs. No doubt Slim and Bear are looking for me, and I'm sure they'll be pissed off when they find out I've been working in the wrong direction. By the time I reach the catwalk, my legs and arms feel like they've had the workout of the century, and my feet are bleeding from the few blisters I opened on the way down the ladder, but I don't waste time in getting back to where I'm supposed to be. I reach sector thirty-six, and collapse to the ground, my legs and feet unwilling to carry me any further. The humming pipes invite me, once again, to close my eyes.

"What the hell do you think you're doing?" Slim barks. "This ain't a damn holiday, Kid."

I open my eyes, my brain fuzzy. Slim is red in the face and looks about ready to slit my throat.

"I must have fallen asleep."

His mouth drops open and his face turns a darker shade of red. "What? You've been napping while I've been scouring these freakin' catwalks like a monkey?"

I get to my feet and try to stretch out the ache in my legs. "No, I-I'm sorry."

"You should be sorry. I missed lunch because I was looking for you. I think you owe me fifty sit-ups."

"But I—"

"Make it one hundred and throw in a few push-ups, too."

"You've got to be kidding me."

Slim gets into my face and growls like a tiger ready to eat its young. "Do I kid about food? Do I?"

Bear laughs behind Slim. "He's your best friend until you steal his sandwich."

"Oh, shut up." Slim turns around and pushes past Bear. He flings his legs over the railing and starts down the ladder to the cement below.

"Did you get your rows inspected?" Bear asks.

"I inspected eleven," I say, withholding which rows. "They're clear."

"I think we're done here, then." He pulls out his new tablet and enters in some information. I wonder if there's anything different about this tablet than his last one. After all, it was a guard's and not an offender's.

"Find anything interesting on that?"

Bear glances at me, and I eye the tablet. He gives me a wink. "I learned what I needed. Let's just keep it at that."

He slips the tablet into his tool bag and climbs onto the ladder. Part of me wants to shake him until he confesses the escape plan. I don't like being left in the dark. It makes me feel that they either don't trust me, or they really don't want me to be a part of it. Then again, if either of those things is true, why did Slim even tell me they had a plan in the first place?

"Kid, you get your skinny butt down here," Slim shouts. "I'm not coming up there again."

Not really wanting to climb down another ladder, I grudgingly obey. As I climb, I think about the locked door I'd found. What's really behind it? Perhaps stairs leading to the stadium seats, a lift that would take me to the control center, or perhaps there's nothing behind it—nothing but an open field without locks or bars. Maybe behind that door is freedom, and all I need is a passkey to find it.

-SEVENTEEN-

BEAR SLAMS ME AGAINST THE FLOOR, AND suddenly he has my head in a death lock. I try to kick out, to break free of his hold, but he has me pinned. I jab my elbow into his ribs, but it feels like striking a wooden beam. I struggle again, this time arching my back until he's forced onto his. Again I jab my elbow, this time lower and up under his ribcage. Finally, he lets go. I scramble off him and get to my feet. The wild look in his eye reminds me he's an offender—an offender who's killed, otherwise he wouldn't be in the Arena. I wonder if anyone's ever been killed in the training room.

I hold my position, fists raised, waiting for him to get up.

"I think the next group battle is a naval fight," I say.

At first he looks surprised. Then his eyebrows scrunch together as if he's angry. "You're supposed to be focusing on training."

"I know. But I've been thinking about the shi—"

Bear swipes my legs out from under me, and I fall to the blue mat with a slap hard enough to force the air from my lungs. He did it so fast I didn't even see it coming.

"Focus," he growls, towering above me.

I get to my feet and once again ready myself; feet apart, hands raised to shoulder level, body turned so that my dominant hand is forward. I really am trying to focus, but I can't get the images of those warships out of my head. For the past three nights during the Choosing, I expected Scarlet Wild would announce a new group battle. I imagined her on one of the ships, bedecked in some outfit that would have been fashionable in the sixteenth century—with the obligatory drooping neckline. But the only things that have been announced are the usual hand-to-hand combats and a couple beast fights. Still, I know it's coming.

There were a dozen ships. All of them man-powered—at least fifty men to a boat just to get them to move. Throw in another ten or twenty on deck for the actual fighting and it would take every last man in the compound. Whatever the game masters are planning is big. It would be the battle of all battles.

But how will it play out? Will they have all the sections against each other? That would be two ships per section. Or maybe they plan on dividing us into two separate armies. There are so many options. I can only guess as to what awaits us in the next few days, and the waiting is making me crazy.

"You're not focusing," Bear snarls. He comes at me with

a right hook, and his fist smashes into my jaw, lifting me off my feet and landing me on the mat—again.

"Ow! That hurt!"

"Imagine if I had a knife in my hand. Now get up!"

It's great that Bear is training me, but I just might die from it. Slim seems to find this all very entertaining. He sits there with his fat butt on the third row, laughing every time I land on my back. Which is a lot. I'd like to see him fight Bear. Now that would be something to laugh at.

I get up from the floor and, for the millionth time that morning, ready myself the way Bear showed me.

He jabs out with his right arm, which I dodge, but he slams me with his left.

"Ow!"

"Stop whining and block me." He strikes out again. Right. Left. Right. Right. His fist catches me in the gut, and I hunch forward. He sighs and pushes me to the ground. "You need to do better."

Slim's bark-like laughter fills the rec room, rousing the attention of the other offenders. I know they see me for what I really am—as much as the media makes me out to be some iconic warrior in the Arena, I'm nothing more than a kid with no talent for fighting.

Bear glares at Slim, then shifts his eyes to me. I can tell I'm driving him crazy, but he's patient—far more patient than any instructor I've ever had in the past.

I tried to learn the cello, once. Mom had been so insistent, and I tried for her, but the tutor swore to heaven I didn't have one ounce of musical talent and threw the cello across the room before turning in his resignation—just minutes into our first lesson. Bear might actually teach me something, if only because he's stuck with me. I wonder what his occupation was before the Arena.

"Show me what you've learned," he says after I get to my feet. "What do you do when I come at you with my right hand?"

Bear moves his fist in slow motion toward my face. I block him with my left hand and push his blow away from me with my right. He comes at me with his left. I block that one too, and throw a wild punch in his direction. He dodges it, grabs my neck, and tosses me to the mat like a rag doll.

"Your punches should come from the center of your body. Stand up and show me how to throw a *real* punch."

I stand again, and Bear waits, ready. I prepare, focus, and throw my punches from my center. I feel like I've done this a hundred times already, but do it again and again. By the time I'm done, my hands are red, my knuckles cracked and bleeding. Bear nods, which I assume means I can take a break. I let out a sigh and turn to Slim.

Out of the corner of my eye, I see Bear flip around, fist barreling toward me. I step back and block his punch with my right hand. He strikes again—I block again. He kicks out with his leg, and I push it away. His next punch flies up toward my chin, but I move to the left, and he just brushes my cheek. Another strike, and I block it. Another, and I duck down.

I steady my legs and throw a punch at his chest. It strikes him in the chin and pain explodes in my hand. I can't help it—I crouch down and clasp my hand to my chest.

Slim's laughter fills my ears. I glare at him while Bear's rare laughter booms through the room. The big, brown man is on his back, rubbing his chin. Did I knock him over? I don't know if I did—I'd been too concerned about my hand.

"Now that's a real punch. Damn, you little shank, you nearly made me bite my tongue off."

Still holding my throbbing hand to my chest, I get to my feet and offer Bear my left. He takes it and I help him up. "I think I broke my hand."

"At least we finally know you can throw a real punch."

Slim claps his hands as he comes down from the bleachers. "I have to admit, that was great. I've always wanted to sock Bear's block off."

"You wanna try it now?" Bear growls.

Slim holds up his hands in surrender. "Whoa! I don't need to. It was better just watching. Come on, Kid. Let's go ice and wrap that hand."

"Are we done, Bear?" I ask.

He smiles and nods. "Unless you want to try for a second shot with your other hand."

I shake my head and follow behind Slim.

HOURS LATER WE SIT IN THE CAFETERIA EATING the last meal of the day. I'm exhausted. Every morning, we start the day with Bear training me, followed by maintenance work, followed by workouts. While I appreciate their efforts to make me a stronger, better fighter, I crave a day off. My hand still hurts when I try to use it, but I didn't break it. Slim assures me I'll be back to normal in a few days.

Tonight's meal is dry, roasted chicken and over-cooked vegetables. I'd consider killing for a steak—a thick, juicy, medium-rare flank. The longer I'm here, the more I realize how good I had it. Senator Gerard had called it a charmed life, and I suppose it was. I don't even recall thanking the cooks and servants that made my meals. I feel bad when I try to think of their names and can't come up with any. The only servant in our household that I ever called by name was Margret, and only because she was our housekeeper and kind of took on the role of matriarch after Mom died.

"Do you ever get tired of the same food over and over?" I ask.

Slim swallows his mouthful. "It's food. I'm surprised you're complaining after your vacation in solitary. What, did they feed you cuisine fit for a senator?"

I shake my head, feeling stupid for saying anything at all. Slim wouldn't understand, and I don't want to try to explain. I'd only end up sounding spoiled. He's right—I should be grateful for what I have, especially after spending two weeks drinking nothing but toilet water. Dry chicken is as good as steak, next to that.

"Another offender has entered the Arena tonight," announced the news anchor. I look up at the screen and see a man, probably in his early twenties, entering the cafeteria. When I realize where he's at, I turn my head and observe him in the flesh.

He looks as I must have, those many weeks ago, scared and worried. He stands motionless at the door. The cafeteria has gone silent, except for the blabbering news anchors.

"Tell us about our newest arrival, Carolyn."

"Thanks, Mark," Carolyn says in a sickly sweet voice. I glance back to the monitor to see a zoomed out scene of the business district. People stand on a grassy knoll, holding hands. "Offender BB8961 was recently charged with the murder of three defectors, after what was supposed to be a peaceful gathering in support for the end of the blue brand turned violent. One of his victims was a five-year-old girl."

A man dashes from the building, firing off a gun into the crowd. People drop to the grass, people scream. A group of men follow behind the gunman, holding anti-defector signs and firing guns into the air.

The group of defectors scatters as the square turns to pandemonium. A team of peace officers, tasers in hand, charge the group of extremists. The gunman goes down, and the camera zooms in, filling the screen with his smiling face.

I turn back to the white-faced, scared man standing in the doorway of the cafeteria. I don't understand how someone who took such pleasure in hurting others can look so terrified now.

"Several of the members of their radical group were taken into custody, but only offender BB8961 was charged with the crime of murder. The others were sentenced to life in the prison mines, with one exception, a female member of the radical group was sentenced to life in the prison fields.

"In related news, Senator Lindt has once again petitioned the senate to instate a protection order for all citizens marked with the blue brand." Carolyn continues to talk about the particulars involved in the protective order, but I can't hear her over the curses the other offenders in the cafeteria are shouting at the new arrival.

"I have a blue brand on me, you shank!" a man shouts. "Why not try to kill me?" More of them join in. Some throw food. Apples, chicken thighs, and potatoes slap against the man's chest. BB8961 lifts his hands and takes a few steps back. A big, burly man with a blue brand on his forearm moves in behind him and pushes him forward. The new offender slides across the floor and crashes into one of the tables. A few men rise and begin kicking him until he scrambles back.

Slim pulls on my arm. "This isn't good. We need to get out of here."

Bear moves to my right and grabs my other arm. They drag me toward the wall while Carolyn, hysterical now, describes what I can't see.

"They're beating him, Mark. I don't understand the savagery …"

Bear and Slim get me to the exit, but I turn to see the man's body being tossed back and forth like a punching bag. He cries for help but no one comes to his aid. The cafeteria is full of animals. They punch, claw, and bite BB8961 with vicious faces.

"Get Kid back to our section and wait there," Bear orders. "They won't stop now they've started."

"What about you?" Slim asks.

"I've got to stop this before the game masters kill us all."

"How do you expect to do that?"

"GO!"

He doesn't need to tell me again, but I look behind me before I duck through the door. The scene has sunk into chaos. One inmate grabs another by his neck and slams his head into the corner of a stainless steel table. He drops to the floor in a pool of blood. More join in the fray.

I turn to Slim and run.

-EIGHTEEN-

AN ALARM BLARES THROUGHOUT THE compound. I fall against the wall and press my hands against my ears. Red lights flash along the ceiling seconds before the wide hall fills with vapor.

"Kid, get up," Slim orders through the piercing sound.

I get to my feet and follow behind Slim as he runs toward Section One's hall, but a wall of vapor pours down on him, and he crumples to the floor. He doesn't move. I back away, turn back toward the cafeteria, but the vapor blocks my path. The nearest hall to my left is clear, so I veer down it and run. I steal a glance back at the atrium and see several offenders rush from the cafeteria, only to fall motionless. *Are they dead? Is this the punishment for violence in the compound? Slim. What about Slim? What about Bear?*

My heart wants me to go back to the atrium and help them, but my mind pushes me further down the hall. I run faster, flying past the line of glass cells. I have to get as far away from the poisonous mist as I can. I enter a rec room at the end of the hall and try to get my bearings. The room is set up similar to Section One's, but the mat in front of the bleachers is red, not blue.

The screen above shows the offenders in the cafeteria choking on the toxic gas. They crash to the floor, some smashing their heads onto the steel benches and tables as they go down. I search for Bear, but I don't see him. What I do see churns my stomach. Blood, and what appears to be the remains of the Arena's newest arrival, litters the floor. I can't fathom the pain he must have felt to be torn limb from limb.

The violent sight pulls at my gut, and I race toward the trash bin next to a rack of barbells. I barely make it in time to empty the contents of my stomach. I dry heave over and over until I'm able to regain control of my body. Somewhere between running into this rec room and throwing up, the alarm stopped. I don't want to, but I sneak a glance back at the monitor.

The scene now shows the news anchors chatting away about the horror that just happened as if it were an everyday occurrence. As if it was just a dramatization put on by very skillful actors. I don't understand how they can disconnect themselves from these men as easily as they do. No matter how animalistic the offenders become, they're still human. No matter the crime offender BB8961 committed—he was still human. He didn't deserve to die like that.

I walk forward and peek down the hallway leading out to the atrium. I don't see the vapor, but that doesn't mean the air down there isn't contaminated. I want to check on Slim. I want to find Bear and make sure he's okay. The panic made me run, but now that everything seems better, all I can think about is how stupid it was for me to leave them. They are my friends—all that I have. If they're dead, I might as well be dead, too.

Determined to do something more than hide away, I go to move but stop. A chill runs up my back and I turn just in time to see two hands reach for me. I drop and roll away, then quickly get to my feet. Slaughter and one of his cronies stare me down, wicked grins stretching their ugly faces. I lift my fists to shoulder height and spread my legs the way Bear taught me. If they want to fight, I'll fight.

"What happened, pretty boy?" Slaughter asks, his eyes darting from me to the monitor. "Were those bad, scary offenders being naughty again?"

Is he really asking me what happened, or is he just taunting me? Either way, I wonder why he and his crony missed the fight. I don't answer, just shift my feet and tighten my fists.

"Looks like they got wiped out by the mist," Crony says. His voice is much too high for a man his size—it's almost comical. Almost. "How long did it take for them to wake up last time? Like a half hour or so?"

Wake up? So the mist isn't poisonous. Relief for my friends helps wash away the guilt of leaving them, but it doesn't help my current situation. I find the exit but Slaughter steps in my path, his sickening grin exposing his blackened teeth and red gums. "Half an hour's long enough for me to have my way with you, pretty boy."

My heart pounds as they both exchange a look. I don't know what unholy thoughts these two men have, but I know I need to get away from here. Slowly they circle around me. I rack my brain for what to do. Bear taught me how to fight a man one-on-one, not two coming at me from either side.

I wait for their strike, trying not to let the fear show. Slaughter's smile is gone, and in its place he wears the expression of a ravenous predator. I dart my eyes back and forth, trying to see which one will attack first. Slaughter nods his head, and they both attack at the same time.

I duck Crony's blow, but Slaughter grabs me around the waist and lifts me up. I throw out my heel and smash it into Crony's face. He drops to the floor, screaming about his nose. My elbow slams into Slaughter's neck and jaw, but he doesn't let go. He flings me back and forth like a rag doll. Suddenly I'm airborne. I crash onto the bleachers and feel the metal seats bruise me to the bone. I try to get up, but Slaughter grabs my ankles. He drags me down the bleachers, making sure I feel every last step. I kick and thrash, trying to get out of his grip, but he laughs at my feeble attempts.

"You're going to like this," he says as he begins pulling at my pants.

"No!" I sit up and pound my fists down on his thick arms. He strikes back, landing a blow on my head that makes it feel as if it will explode. My neck slams onto the bottom step of the bleachers and the lights in the room flicker in and out of focus. He drags me across the floor.

The room is blurry, and all I can see is the red of the mat and the shadows of two men standing above me. One of the shadows drops toward my head. Pain shoots through my shoulders as Crony pins my arms under his knees. He grabs my shirt and rips it open. He licks my chest with his sticky tongue and I scream and scream. I struggle with all my might to get him off me. I can't let this happen. I'd rather face a thousand saber-tooths than this. Anything but this.

I can't help but think of Slim's story about his friend in the prison mines. How he found Danny at the bottom of a shaft after he'd been beaten and raped. I didn't want to be Danny. I don't want that to happen to me. They can kill me, but I won't let them touch me.

Slaughter laughs as he tears at my pants. He comes at me, and I kick. My heel finds his groin, and Slaughter growls, hunching forward. I try to lift my body free of Crony, but he presses down even harder. I sink my teeth into his arm. Bitter blood fills my mouth. Crony screams, and his weight shifts. I push up and roll. I get to my feet, but am pulled back down. Slaughter climbs atop me and slaps my face over and over.

"NO! Get off me! GET OFF ME!"

He flips me onto my stomach and for a moment all I hear is my own ragged breathing while he fumbles with his own pants. I scream and he presses my face into the mat so my teeth cut into my mouth and any sound I make is muffled. I try to breathe through my nose, but I do nothing but suck in blood. *Let me die. Let me die.* I shut my eyes and repeat the mantra, trying to remove my mind from this moment in time.

Slaughter groans and his body drops down on mine, pressing me into the mat. I thrash about, trying to get free of his weight. His drool drips down my neck and runs under my chest, but I'm able to scramble forward and he doesn't pull me back. He just lies there, unmoving. I don't care why—I crawl forward and steal a glance behind me.

Slaughter lies face-down on the mat. The back of his head is smeared with blood, but he's not dead. I'm not lucky enough for that. His back rises and falls as he breathes. Behind him, Slim kneels on the floor, a bloody barbell resting in his lap. Crony lies on his back near him, his blank eyes staring off into nothing.

Slim's eyes connect with mine, but he doesn't seem to see me. His gaze is filled with sorrow and regret. He lets go of the barbell and it rolls off his lap and hits the floor with a clank.

"I didn't save Danny. I didn't save him." His chin quivers, and a sob escapes his lips.

I crawl toward my friend and grab his hand. "No, you didn't. You didn't save Danny, but you saved me. Slim, you saved me!"

For a long time we stay like that. We don't talk. We just cry. We both cry for Danny. Although I never met him, I feel like I'm connected to him through Slim. I know the panic and fear that must've filled Danny's mind before he was tossed to the bottom of that pit. I don't judge Slim one bit for avenging Danny's death. Men like Slaughter and Crony deserve to die. But could I do what Slim did? Take a life to protect someone I love? Is it wrong to kill in order to stop an evil act? Or is it all evil?

My eyes flick to the barbell, blood staining its polished silver surface. It would be so easy to finish the job Slim started. I could lift the barbell and, with one blow, remove any threat of Slaughter hurting me, or any other person, in this world. It would be so easy.

Without even realizing it, I have the barbell in my hands. I stand over Slaughter and think about the ugliness he brings to the world. I would be doing everyone a favor by removing his very existence. *It would be so easy.*

I lift the barbell. The weight of it pulls on my biceps and makes my shoulder muscles burn, but soon I won't feel them. Once I drop the bar, the weight of it will be gone—just as easy as that.

Slim is suddenly next to me, but he doesn't take the barbell from me. I'm not sure why I hesitate, though. Slaughter has done nothing but kill—and he wanted to kill me. Slim touches my shoulder.

"Don't become him," he whispers. "Don't become me."

"You're nothing like him! He kills and likes it. He'll try again. I know he'll try again."

"Life is a gift, Cal. You were put on this earth to give it, not take it away. I won't let you become something you're not."

My name! He said my name! I close my eyes and tears fall to my cheeks. I'd almost forgotten who I am. For a strange, confusing, otherworldly moment I forgot I'm not a killer. I will never be like Slaughter.

I lower the barbell and Slim takes it from me. I feel the hate leave me as Slim drops the weight to the mat. I reach for my pants, but they're a torn mess. Slim pulls off his shirt, and I wrap it around my waist.

We don't talk as we walk together back to Section One. We pass men slowly waking from the vapor's spell. They seem confused, and most of them look as bad as I feel. With the adrenaline now wasted, I realize the extent of the beating I took at Slaughter's hands. I hurt everywhere. Slim helps me to the showers, then treats the cuts and bruises when I'm finished. All the while, he's silent as he cares for me, as a father would—a father I wish I had.

Offenders begin to trickle into our section, but they're still recovering from the effects of the vapor. Some cut curious glances our way, but no one escaped the chaos in the cafeteria unscathed.

The trumpet of the Choosing echoes through the hall. It's time for Scarlet Wild to announce the fights for this evening. With our reward time working maintenance over, any of us could be selected for a battle.

With a groan, I get to my feet and lean on Slim the whole way into the rec room.

Only a few offenders sit on the bleachers. I assume most are still waking up from the vapor. Either that or they're dead. I search for Bear, but I haven't seen him since we left him at the cafeteria. Worry eats at me as I wait.

The trumpet calls again, and my eyes are drawn to the monitor. The logo of the Arena spins, and an ocean tidal wave crashes behind it, sending a huge spray of water into the air. My stomach clenches, and I turn to Slim. I can tell from the look in his eyes he understands—they're going to be announcing the group battle.

The screen fades to a scene of the ocean. A galley ship, with twenty-five manned oars on each side, slashes through the waves. At the bow stands Scarlet Wild, dressed exactly how I imagined in a bejeweled gown from the mid-sixteenth century with a neckline revealing her ample cleavage. Atop her head is a feathered tricorn hat and in her hand, a silver rapier. She holds the rapier high above her and beams her white teeth at the camera.

"Before the industrial age, ships were moved across the waters by the power of men, and by the power of men, we conquered the world. Join us in one week as the Arena brings you a battle the likes of which has never been seen since the time before the atomic wars. Watch as all offenders in the Arena battle to the death in a naval competition. We promise you—this will be a show to remember."

"Did she just say *all* offenders?" a man behind us asks.

I knew this would happen. The only way to move that many ships was to use us all. This would be a fight to remember, all right. Half or more of us won't survive.

"To make the fight even more fantastic," Scarlet continues, "the senate will award the victorious offenders with a grand prize."

Prize? What reward could the senate offer any of these men? I shake all wandering thoughts from my head and focus on Scarlet.

"The offenders shall be sectioned off into two teams, the Hawks and the Falcons. Each offender on the winning team will be entered into a lottery." Scarlet pauses for dramatic effect and the camera zooms in on her now-serious face. "The winner of the lottery will be given a full pardon by the senate and shall return to life outside the Arena."

-NINETEEN-

NO ONE SPEAKS WHEN THE SCREEN GOES black. No one even moves. The game masters have just given a way for one of us to leave, to return to a normal life. It's almost too good to be true. Could an offender simply walk out of the Arena and be thrown back into society without any type of reformation? Perhaps that's what the game masters want—to release a killer only to have him murder again. They probably assume he'd be returned to the system in short order and in reality they'd lose nothing. Except for one innocent life.

Could this be my way out? I know Bear and Slim are planning an escape, but this could truly be the way out. Maybe this is Senator Gerard's idea—he provided the ships, after all. Perhaps he did have my best interests in mind. He had to know I could never have been capable of killing my father. All that talk about my cry for attention would just prove he had nothing to do with me winning the lottery. He couldn't look like he'd set things up. The senate wouldn't allow such tampering with the Arena. But maybe he somehow fixed this whole thing?

Then again, how could he guarantee my safety during the battle? How could he ensure that my team would win?

Slim is as silent as the rest of us, and I wonder if he's thinking the same things I am, or if his brain is now working out the best attack plan. He's probably laying out a grid of toilet paper boats in his mind.

"Stop smiling like you think this is your ticket home," he whispers.

I didn't realize I *had* been smiling. I force my lips together and give my best frown. Slim shakes his head and strides across the rec room. With what I've just been through, the last thing I want to do is climb. I stay put for a few seconds. Slim is half way up the wall by the time I get there. Even though it hurts, I follow. By the time I get to the top, my heart is pumping and my muscles actually feel better. Maybe a workout really does help ease the pain.

"Okay, Captain, what's your plan?" I pull my legs over the top of the platform. Slim scowls at me like I'm a student in a classroom asking a lot of stupid questions. I shrug, hoping he'll just get on with whatever he wanted to talk to me about. When he still says nothing, I follow his gaze—Bear has finally returned. Without talking to anyone, he heads toward the climbing wall and starts up. He has a few visible cuts and bruises, but otherwise looks as healthy as ever. I'm glad to see he made it out of the cafeteria in one piece. I can't stand the thought of losing him—or Slim. If the lottery really is my ticket home, what about Slim and Bear? How could I leave them in here while I go free?

Bear gets to the top and his eyes bulge when he sees the bandages covering my body. He fixes an angry glare at Slim. "What the hell happened to him? I said to get him back to the damn section."

"Slaughter happened to him," Slim says quietly.

I can't read Bear's expression. He stares at me until heat rises in my cheeks. I don't know why I'm embarrassed, but I am. Maybe he's pissed that I couldn't fight him off? I can see rage in his eyes, for me or Slaughter, I don't know. I also see something like sadness, but I'm not sure what to think of that.

"You okay?"

I nod and try not to think about what happened. "I don't want to talk about it. I expect you both want to talk about Scarlet's latest announcement."

"I don't buy it," Bear says flatly.

Slim harrumphs. "You and everyone else in this compound. Well, with the exception of smiley face there." He nods toward me.

What the heck did I do?

"You wanna tell me what else I missed?" Bear asks.

"The kid thinks this lottery is his ticket home."

I start to object, but Slim isn't wrong. I did think this was my ticket home.

Slim rolls his eyes. "Why does every teenager in the world think they're the center of the universe? You think just because they offer a way out, you're the one who gets it? What makes you any different from the other men in this hell hole?"

"Shut your blower, Slim," Bear orders.

"Do you think I'm the only one who saw that smile when Scarlet announced the lottery? You might as well have gotten up and shouted to the other men down there that you were on your way out of here. Perhaps followed it up with some kind of victory dance?"

Slim's words make me tense. So what? I *do* think the lottery is a set up to get me out of here. Slim said I was different, and he's right. I'm different from the other men in this compound because I'm the only innocent one. Why can't he see all the pieces like I do?

"Didn't you see who paid for those galleys?" I asked. "They had Gerard's name all over them. Why would he provide those ships and then have them offer a lottery?"

Slim rolls his eyes. "Kid, how many times do I have to tell you to use your freakin' brain? What do you think those men will do to you if you start strutting around like you already won? You saw what happened in the cafeteria. You'll be next … and I won't be able to stop them."

I can't help it; I look down at the men in the rec room. They are too far away, but sudden paranoia makes them appear to be looking up at me with vengeance in their eyes.

Maybe Slim is right. Maybe I am acting like I'm the center of the universe. Maybe I'm totally wrong about Gerard and the lottery.

"I say we stick to the original plan," Slim whispers. "I, for one, don't believe the Arena would let any of us go. They won't hold up their end of the bargain. I know you want to think your darling senator friend has your back, but that guy is as slick as they come. My gut says he's the very shank who killed your daddy."

What? Gerard? He was my dad's best friend. He always took care of our family, especially after Mom died. Slim was right about a lot of things but he is wrong about this. Gerard couldn't possibly have killed Dad. What did he have to gain by it? And why would he pin it all on me? That just didn't make sense. Slim doesn't know Gerard like I do.

"You think about it, Kid, then get back to me. Right now we need to discuss our exit plan. Bear, I trust you got what you needed from that tablet?"

"It's all here." Bear pats the pouch at his side that holds the tablet. "I actually think the best time to do this is during the naval battle."

I sigh, making sure they hear the irritation in it. "Are you guys going to let me in on this grand scheme, or am I just supposed to follow along?"

"That depends," Slim says. "Are you going to go off all smiles and celebrations if we do?"

"I'm not an idiot."

"Really? You surprised me just a minute ago with how idiotic you can be."

"That's enough," Bear growls. "You two need to get over yourselves. We only have a week to get this put into place. I was hoping for more time."

Bear pauses and eyes me, as if gauging my trustworthiness. Frustration lurches in my gut. Why should I have to prove myself? They've been so elusive—maybe they should worry about *me* trusting *them.*

The emergency exit pops into my mind, and I feel the blush of embarrassment heat my face again. I guess I'm not the only one keeping secrets.

"If we tell you what we have to do, you might not want any part of it," Slim admits.

"If it gets me out of here, I want in." They both look at me as if weighing me in their minds. Slim's eyes rest on my forearm. There's nothing there but a small hint of a scratch I got while fighting the saber-tooth. "What are you looking at?"

Slim cringes then says, "Say we can get out of the Arena. Say Bear and I have the perfect way to escape the actual building. What happens after that?"

"We go find Mary. I'm sure her dad can help us—he's the leader of the blue brands. Maybe they can hide us away. Maybe we could even sneak back into my house and look for clues to who killed my—"

"You seem to be forgetting something." Slim taps my forearm with a fat finger. I look down, but still don't get what he's so worried about. He turns to Bear and whispers, "And you thought he was smart."

"Shut up. I don't know what you're fishing for. And why do you keep tapping my freakin' arm?"

"We all have them, Kid." Slim waits for me to connect the dots. We all have arms? We all have what? Then reality smacks me in the head. I rarely ever think about it because it was embedded in my arm when I was a baby. My tracker. Of course! How could we leave the Arena with a tracker in our arms? The second we escaped, they'd find us. They both smile and I can tell they know I've figured it out. No wonder they didn't want to talk about escaping—it's impossible.

"Why are we even talking about it, then?" I ask, a little angry, a whole lot discouraged.

"Did you ever wonder what Bear did before he was brought to live in this five star resort?" Slim asks.

I shrug. "I figured he was a teacher or something. He's good at instructing and leading."

"Bear was a freakin' doctor."

"Then what are you doing in here?" I ask. Bear doesn't meet my eyes. "If you're a doctor you saved lives not ended them."

"It's not something I'm proud of, and I don't tell just anyone." His eyes finally meet mine and I recognize the same regret in them that I saw in Slim's after he killed Crony. Silence hangs between us and I wonder if he's going to say anything more. I can tell Slim knows the truth; his eyes are fixated on Bear, as if silently urging him to continue.

Finally Bear lets out a breath. "I wasn't just a doctor. I was a surgeon."

"The best in all of Primus," Slim adds.

"I don't need any help telling *my* story." Bear glares hard at Slim before continuing. "I fixed up all sorts of people. They'd come in with heart problems, lung problems, the basic fixer-uppers. I fixed them all. About eleven years ago, I got a rather special patient. She had a condition we hadn't seen since the atomic wars. You see back then, they had a cure for it, but we didn't have it anymore—one of a million treatments that were lost to war."

My stomach tightens. I knew someone who died eleven years ago from a disease that was uncommon in our time. My hands start to shake. I'm not sure I want to hear the rest of Bear's story. I'm afraid of where it might lead.

Bear goes on. "I thought that if we removed the infected area, perhaps we'd eliminate the threat to her whole body. You see, I was trying to save her life. Many of my colleagues thought we should try several rounds of nanorobotics, but back then, they were still in experimental stages, and I don't think they could have done much to stop the cancer from spreading."

Cancer. He said the word that had turned my whole world upside down from the time I was five years old. That horrible word had turned my home into a lonely prison. My father went from a caring, nurturing parent to an absent workaholic and a stickler for following the letter of the law. I hated that word—cancer—more than anything in the world.

"After the surgery, things looked promising. At first, I thought she'd pull through—but then things turned bad. They turned bad real fast. When she died, her husband and others blamed me for her death. They said I experimented with unknown procedures and mutilated her body because she no longer had her breasts. My trial was one of the swiftest and clumsiest I've seen—until yours, that is. And here I am. Trying to survive." Bear pauses. His eyes glisten with unshed tears but he doesn't look away. "I was sent here for killing your mother, Calvin. I tried to save her—I tried everything I knew, everything I could imagine."

It's the second time today someone has said my name, and I should've been grateful to hear it. Instead my whole soul is filled with bitterness. *No wonder Bear hated me from the moment I entered the compound. My father's the one who put him here.*

He looks at me with longing eyes, waiting for me to give some sort of reply, but I say nothing. I glare at Slim who avoids my eyes.

"You knew," I say, my words filled with betrayal. "You knew and yet you said nothing."

"I—"

"No! I don't want to hear another thing from you." I get up and swing my legs over the platform. The pain returns to my body, but I use it to fuel my anger. Bear reaches a hand toward me but I swat it away. "Don't touch me! Because of you my childhood was a living hell! My father hated me. You wanna know why? Because he said I reminded him too much of her and not enough of him; because I liked history and textbooks like she did and could care less about the government. He hated me because I was there and she wasn't. I wouldn't be here if it weren't for you. And *you*! You knew all along and you never told me. You let me be all buddy-buddy with the man that killed my mom? How sick is that?"

I start climbing down the wall. Slim leans over the wall. "It's not like that, Cal. You have to start listening instead of shouting accusations. We're trying to save your freakin' life. Can't you see that we're the good guys here?"

"Good guys don't kill!"

The look in their eyes says I've crossed the line. I've lumped them in with all the other men in the compound like Slaughter. But isn't that what they are—killers?

They call for me to return, but I ignore them. My feet hit the floor and I run. I run to find solitude in a place where none exists.

-TWENTY-

TWO DAYS HAVE PASSED SINCE SCARLET WILD'S announcement about the lottery, and the anxious looks in the offenders' eyes as I pass them in the halls seem to increase each day. Everyone wants to win that ticket to freedom. Luckily, no one but Slim seems to have caught my grin on the day of the Choosing. They treat me no differently than they treat each other.

I keep mostly to myself, avoiding Slim and Bear at all costs. I don't need friends like them, friends that keep such dark secrets from me. They try to talk to me by hanging out at the ends of halls or waiting by the food counter, but I quickly shoot them down or skirt around them. I even find a new cell to sleep in. With so many men dying in the brawl in the cafeteria, empty cells are easy to come by.

Slaughter recovered from his head injury, and I'm sure he won't pass at a chance to seek his revenge. I've taken to sitting with Fist and Hammer at meal times, only to keep men with muscle close by.

I'm not worried for Slim's safety. Slaughter was hit from

behind, and I doubt he knows who got the better of him. The only thing I'm sure of is that he remembers me.

Sections One through Three have joined together as part of the Hawks team. After very little debate, Bear is elected our leader. I'm not surprised—he's been around the longest out of anyone in our sections. Slim sticks to him like a shadow, and I know he's probably come up with some battle plan we'll all be hearing about soon. The other sections are grouped into the Falcons' team and choose none other than Slaughter to lead them. It seems fitting that men like that have the name Falcons. I'm pretty sure falcons are the only species of bird that preyed solely on other birds.

After my morning meal, I sneak away to exercise by myself. A corner in the training room serves me well. Bear has most of the men using the weights, working on rowing, or practicing hand-to-hand. Here, I'm left alone. I can't decide if I like it. I feel more alone than I did when I was in solitary, but I can't bring myself to let anyone else in. As long as I don't start talking to the walls again, I'll be fine, right? Soon I'll win the lottery and be home and this will all be just a bad memory.

I hate to admit it to myself, but my heart is broken. I truly looked up to Bear and Slim. They'd been my friends—more than that, they were my brothers. Every time I think about what Bear did, I feel sick to my stomach. Why did he let her die? Why didn't they tell me sooner?

I lie down on my back and lift my legs up onto the wall.

I take one quick breath and begin attacking my abdomen with crunches. The one thing the Arena has given me is a body a kid my age would only dream of having. I no longer resemble the skinny nobody who was sentenced to this hell zone—now my muscles bulge in all the right spots and I can hold my own in a fight. When I reach one hundred crunches, I flip over and work on push-ups. These still hurt my shoulders a bit from Slaughter and Crony's handiwork, but I know the workout will soon drive the pain of that away. I need the pain to go away. Every time I feel it, I remember the terror of that day. It was a miracle Slim got to me before they'd finished their evil deeds.

Slim. I swear there isn't a minute that goes by that I don't think of him. My eyes sting, and I flip over and start on crunches again. I don't want to cry. Crying is a weakness, and it only shows self-pity. Yet isn't that what I'm doing? Throwing a one-man pity party for myself, all because Slim kept a secret from me? It isn't as though I haven't kept secrets from him. Never once did I tell him about the emergency exit, the ladder, or the door. At least when they told me about Bear, they were coming clean.

"Ugh!" I hate considering they might not be in the wrong. Bear freaking killed my mother, and Slim knew about it. I can't make that fact go away or change it to be something it's not.

I get to my feet and decide to jog along the perimeter of the training room. I need to clear my head. I need to think about something other than Slim and Bear.

I'm on my second lap when Fist shouts for me to join everyone in the rec room. I raise my hand in acknowledgement, but take my time following him out. I'm sure this is when Bear will give us our orders. He'll tell us what we'll all do during the naval battle, and I know every last one of them will be listening. They all want to win a chance of being entered into that lottery. Taking my time, because I'm still trying to avoid Bear, I cross the training room and do a few stretches before entering the rec room. When I do, every eye is on me.

Maybe I should've followed Fist out right away. All the offenders from team Hawk sit on the bleachers or stand lined up around the room. Bear and Slim stand in the center of the group and glare at me like I'm a disobedient child.

"Now that we're *all* here," Bear says, narrowing his eyes at me, "we can begin discussing the details of our attack plan."

Heat flares on my face and I know I'm as red as an apple. I spot Fist and squeeze into a seat between him and Hammer. We're so crammed our legs are touching—Hammer's bony hip grinds into mine, but he doesn't complain, so I don't, either. We all look up at our commander, awaiting his orders.

Bear pulls out his tablet, the very tablet he swindled out of a guard's grasp. What information did he get from that tablet? Part of me wonders if I should stop ignoring them so they can get me out of here. Bear said the naval battle would be the best chance of their escape plan working—I still didn't know what it is, but I do want my freedom. But I'm positive Gerard's donation of the galleys and the lottery has to be connected. I know he wants me out of here as much as I do.

Slim's words about Gerard filter back into my mind: *My gut says he's the very shank who killed your daddy.* He told me to think on it, but I haven't. Ever since the revelation about Bear's past, that's all I've thought about. For Slim, it seemed to make sense that Gerard would kill Dad, but most people only kill because they're motivated to do so. What motivation could have led Gerard to kill his best friend?

My thoughts flutter to other possible suspects—like perhaps Senator Lindt, who was made Consul—but now really isn't the time. As much as I want to figure out who killed my father, I have to focus on staying alive. No matter how angry I am at Bear and Slim, right now, they're the ones to lead the Hawks to a victory. And I have to be victorious.

Bear taps on his tablet, and the monitor above the bleachers lights up with a picture of one of the galleys. "This is one of our six ships. You will note that each ship has fifty oarsmen to power it. Those oarsmen need to be strong and resilient. They can't be quitters. If the ship can't move, we can't fight. Don't make me explain the meaning of a sitting duck. If you haven't guessed already, the men who've been working on rowing the past two days are our oarsmen."

A few groans rumble through the crowd. Bear holds up a hand. "I don't want to hear any whining, whimpering or sorry-sissy-crying! Act like men or we'll treat you like little girls and find you some dolls to play dress up with."

The room falls silent and several of the men straighten up. Including myself.

"Don't worry. You'll all get your chance to fight. Learn to use your oar as a weapon. In the morning, we'll be getting a few dozen to practice with. You'll find they're extremely heavy, but I'm sure you'll get the hang of them. Just remember your number one purpose is to see that we move on that water.

"The rest of you will be fighting. As you can see, there won't be much room for us to move around, with the oarsmen taking up the majority of the deck space. There will be some pushing and shoving and probably some uncomfortable moments for all of us. Get over that now. Those assigned to the deck will be working on hand-to-hand combat as well as sword fighting and manning cannons."

Several murmurs ripple through the room. Bear clears his throat, quieting the men. "Yes, there will be cannons on the galleys, but only two per vessel. They're located at the bow—that's the front of the ship. I have been notified the cannons are the only firearms that will be permitted in this battle. Although this is supposed to be a reenactment of the Battle of Lepanto, the game masters have made a few changes to the actual historical accounts. That doesn't matter because I doubt any of you remember being taught this particular battle in school—I'm sure half of you didn't even attend school. We'll only be allowed arrows, spears, swords, and knives. Which means if we want to have any chance at beating those sorry shanks on Falcon, we'll have to get our galleys alongside theirs and board them one by one. Once aboard, we fight it out."

Bear doesn't go into any more details on the attack plan. He just sorts us into different groups, having all the oarsmen work together in Section Three, all good swordsmen practicing in Section Two and the rest of us in Section One.

I've never held a bow and arrow in my life, but he assigns me to a group of fifteen archers. I follow them into a special training room next to the weapons vault. It's long, narrow, and dimly lit. Twenty stalls line one half of the room, each stall with a wooden bow, quiver of arrows, and a target in the shape of a man. I take the stall at the very end of the room, not wanting the other men to see how bad I am.

I pick up the bow and feel it in my hands. It's heavier than it looks and feels awkward in my hands. I pick up an arrow and touch the tip to my finger. It's as dull as a marble. I half expected it to be sharp. Then again, if someone knew what they were doing this arrow could kill. Why would the game masters allow us real weapons to work with? What would prevent any of these men from using these on each other?

My answer comes immediately as one of the archers at the front of the room turns to leave with his bow and quiver in hand. There's a flash and a pop, and the offender flies across the room, slamming into the wall. Some of the men laugh. Others shake their heads and comment on his stupidity. It takes him a good two minutes before he gets to his feet. He staggers around, looking drunk more than anything, a slight wisp of smoke trailing out from his singed hair. I almost laugh.

I turn back to my stall and do my best to place the arrow in the bowstring. I try three times before I finally manage to get it to stay in place. I have no idea why Bear thought I'd be a good archer. So far, I suck. The room fills with whooshes and thunks. I look down the line at the other men who seem to have no problem nocking their arrows and hitting their targets. The offender closest to me, an ugly man from Section Three, eyes me. I can tell he's weighing me up, trying to determine who'd win if it ever came to a fight between us. His constant stare, with his dark eyes and thin pierced lips, makes warning bells sound in the back of my mind. He's waiting to see what I'm made of, and I have to show him I know what I'm doing. The horrible reality of it is, I don't.

I nock the arrow and pull back on the bowstring. The muscles in my arm flinch and my elbow shakes as I hold the string taut. I release the arrow and the bowstring whips back, giving me an instant welt on my arm. Pain ricochets up my forearm and around my wrist. I drop the bow. It lands next to my arrow that for some reason decided to go with gravity instead of going for the target. A snigger pulls my eyes to the offender from Section Three. He grins at me, his grizzly mouth filled with overcrowded yellow teeth. He winks and pulls back on his own bowstring. A slight wiz follows the arrow as it plunges into his target. Ugly turns back to me and blows a kiss.

His cockiness reminds me of Slaughter, and rage fills my insides. I've got to get out of here. Hands balled into fists, I move toward the exit. Just as I'm about to pass Ugly, he steps in my way. His tongue sneaks past his crooked teeth, licking his lips. "You don't have to go. I thought we could get to know each other. A little boy like you should have a daddy."

"Out of my way," I order.

His grin fades, replaced by a sneer. I step forward again and he goes to touch my neck. I slap his hand away and push my fist into his chest. He stumbles back, knocking over his quiver. At that second I want to pound his face in but I don't waste my time. I march past and head out the door. Archery sucks, and I don't want to try anymore. I'll take my chances doing something else.

Five minutes later, Slim finds me hiding in the corner of the training room doing crunches. "I admire your sudden affection for your abs, Kid, but it doesn't look like archery to me."

"This is something I can do," I spit. "You know as well as I do I can't shoot an arrow. Why did you give me a stupid task? Do you think I can't fight with a sword? I'd be better at that than trying to shoot an arrow."

He laughs. "The bowstring gotcha, did it?"

"It's not funny. I have a welt the size of your mother's butt on my arm."

"Hey-hey, you best not be talking about my mama. Only friends can get away with a joke like that, and last time I checked, you were avoiding me like you would a beast fight."

I sit up and stare at his feet. I'm not ready to talk things out, but I can't avoid him forever. We only have a few days until we head back into the Arena—what if he dies in there? I remember the way I felt the last time I thought he was dead. I'm not sure I can go through that again.

"Why didn't you tell me sooner?" I ask before I can talk myself out of it.

Slim looks around the room, trying to determine if we'll be overheard. He sits down next to me. "We all learn things we'd rather not, Cal."

I'm once again thrown by the use of my real name. It feels good to hear, to know I am still me. "Hiding from the truth doesn't make it go away. Whether we'd told you now or weeks ago, the pain would be the same."

"I trusted him. How can I trust a man I know killed—?"

"Stop that!" Slim points a finger in my face. "You get off your sorry bus right now, Kid. That man did everything he could to save your mama. She had cancer, man. Cancer! Now I know you're a bright kid. Surely you studied some of that during your time in school. Before the atomic wars, it killed millions of people. It didn't care if you were white, black, red, or polka dot. You could have been male, female, old, young, rich or poor, it still took you, and there was nothing anyone could do about it. Cancer killed your mama. Don't blame a man for trying to save what couldn't be saved."

"Cancer's to blame, eh? If cancer's to blame, why did they send him here?"

"Damn it, Calvin! What good is a brain like yours if you refuse to freakin' use it? Your daddy was a senator—*a senator*! He was grief-stricken and he needed a person to blame. Why not the doctor who couldn't save her?" His statement hangs in the air, and I know he's right. Deep down I've known all along, but it was so easy to blame Bear, blame him for everything that had gone wrong. Slim sighs, then says, "Although from what Bear says, it wasn't your daddy pressing the issue. Someone else made that trial what it was."

"Who pressed the trial then?"

"Ten guesses," Slim teases. I give him an elbow to the side and he goes on. "When you look at it from my angle, you begin to see many similarities between your trial and the trial of the once Doctor Barrett Otis. You see there's a certain senator who happens to hold a lot of sway in legal affairs because he owns one of the largest sources of money in Primus. Come to think of it, he's the only senator that has income outside the senate … have you guessed his name yet?"

"Senator Gerard," I whisper. Saying his name somehow feels like betrayal. I still don't think Gerard could be capable of so many wicked things. Would he have sent a man to the

Arena just because he could? Did he really have that much power? "But why? Why would he do any of it?"

"Ah! The *why*! Now that is the most important question when it comes to solving a mystery. Find out the *why,* so it all makes sense. Find out the *why,* and you have your answers."

I stare down at my feet, trying to see the connections the way Slim did, but I can't get past the fact that Senator Gerard was like an uncle to me. As long as I can remember, he's always been around. Even when Dad wasn't there, Gerard was. I close my eyes and I can almost see him and Mom out in the garden, when he helped build the pergola. I shake the thought from my head. That has been Dad who helped build the pergola … hadn't it?

Slim slaps my leg, pulling me from my thoughts. "Come on, Kid, we still have hours left to train, and someone needs to show you the proper way to shoot an arrow."

-TWENTY-ONE-

TWO HOURS INTO SLIM'S INSTRUCTION ON HOW to handle a bow and arrow, I'm as done as when I started. Archery sucks. My forearm has turned purple from the bowstring hitting me so often and my aim hasn't improved at all. I think I have a better chance getting hit with an arrow than shooting one. But at Slim's insistence, I give it one last go.

I nock an arrow and pull the bowstring back. I release it, and the string whops me again. The arrow flops to the ground, barely jumping two feet from where I stand. I let out a groan and rub the pain from my forearm.

Slim doesn't even attempt to hide his joy at my expense. His laughter fills the room, pulling the other archers' attention to me.

Ugly from Section Three eyes me again and I repay him with a scowl. He takes the hint and turns back to his own target. Men behind him laugh along with Slim and I grind my teeth. *Great! Now I look like an even bigger idiot in front of everyone.*

"I told you I was bad."

"Bad?" Slim snickers. "Boy, you are downright awful."

"Stop laughing."

"Maybe you should just try throwing the arrow, instead."

Ugly sniggers loudly, and I secretly want to shoot an arrow at him just to make him shut up. Knowing that would only provide more embarrassment, I toss the bow at Slim and leave.

He catches up with me in the training room. "Kid, you take things too serious. Archery takes time. You need to relax."

"Pull me off archery. I can't hit a target even if my life depends on it."

Slim's smile vanishes and his voice is suddenly soft. "What if your life did depend on it?"

"What are you talking about?"

He puts a finger to his lips. "Let's just say that Bear needs you on deck as an archer. You'll be assigned to our galley."

"Why can't I be assigned sword fighting? Let Hammer work with me. I'm sure in a couple days I'd be fine—"

"Kid, you're not listening. You *are* assigned archery. Archers don't board other ships, fighters do. Now get your sorry shank back in there and practice what I showed you. I have to go check in with Bear."

I try to argue, but his stare reminds me too much of my father's. They both have that same deep brow when they mean business. So, Slim and Bear want me on deck, but not fighting, and nothing I say or do will change their minds. I drop my shoulders and begin sulking back to the archery room.

"Hey, Kid," Slim shouts. I turn and see something fly toward me. I reach up and snatch it from the air. "Try that on. I'd have given it to you sooner, but you needed to learn what happens when you don't hold the bow right."

He laughs and I look down. It's a leather guard for my wrist. I wish I had the skill of the best archer in the world because at that moment, I wanted to use Slim's big butt for target practice.

THE WRIST GUARD HELPS MAKE LEARNING more bearable. At least when the bowstring slaps against my forearm it doesn't hurt. However, I still can't come close to hitting my target. I close my eyes and take slow, deep breaths. I've got to get this down. Slim made it seem like my life really did depend on being able to shoot an arrow.

The room has grown quiet since the other offenders went to lunch. My stomach growls but I tell myself I can't leave until I've managed to at least hit the target. Food can wait until later.

I follow through with what Slim taught me. I place three fingers under the arrow and draw the bowstring back, keeping my arm taut and my elbow high. I let the string rest against my cheek, the fletching tickling my nose as I hold the arrow still, preparing to shoot. I take in a deep breath and hold it in, biting down on my lower lip. I line the tip of the arrow up with my target and let go at the same time I release the air in my lungs. I bring my hand back behind me and the arrow flies forward—and finds its target. It enters a good six inches below where I planned, but it actually hit the target!

I don't hesitate. I grab another arrow and do the same. With each new release the arrow comes closer and closer to the target and my confidence grows. I let loose another set of arrows, and each finds its mark. My stomach rumbles, and I'm quickly pulled from the excitement of finally figuring out how to shoot. I need food.

I jog down the hallway into the cafeteria just in time to see the food disappear under the counter. Hammer and Fist look up from their barren plates and laugh. It's always fun to see others suffer, even those you call your friends. I shrug like I don't care if I won't eat for another twelve hours. I must be a bad actor because they only laugh harder. I shake my head and turn around. I might as well do something productive with my time rather than sulk about missing my meal.

I take two steps, and come face to face with Slaughter.

"Well, well, if it isn't the pretty boy." His one eye glares at me as his tongue flicks over his lips. "Did you miss meal time? I have something to fill you up."

"Buzz off!" I try to sidestep him, but he plants his feet firmly in front of mine.

"I don't remember how far I got with you last time, but I promise you, I'll remember the next."

My hands slam into his rock hard chest, and he steps back. "You didn't get anywhere. And there will *never* be a next time. You'll never touch me again!"

He takes a step forward and I can smell the roasted chicken on his breath. Suddenly all my hunger has vanished. He doesn't reach for me, only stares with that one dark eye. "Oh, I'll be touchin'. One day, I will."

Why didn't I kill him when I had the chance? I knew that he'd never give up. For him I was nothing more than prey, a special kind of kill he wanted stuffed and mounted on his wall.

"I should've killed you." I say it without thinking—I didn't want him to know I had the chance and didn't take it. That I wasn't strong enough to kill when I could have. When I should have.

He smiles, his gums red and his teeth black. "Your mistake."

"A mistake I won't make again." I bring my head up, leveling my nose with his. "It gets chaotic in group battles. Anything can happen."

His one eye narrows and I wonder if he remembers the first threat he ever made to me. His size and cruelty still scare me, but I have to be brave. I spared his life before, but if it comes down to him or me again, I won't let anything hold me back. I don't want to become a killer, but I won't ever let him hurt me again. I won't be his, or anyone's, victim.

I give him another shove and step around him when he backs up. I don't turn around, but I hear the murmurs of the offenders who must have seen our little exchange. I half expect to feel a blow to the back of my head or a kick to my legs—but Slaughter does nothing.

I feel him staring after me with his one ugly eye as I walk away. Probably planning our next meeting in the naval battle. I have three days to perfect my archery.

-TWENTY-TWO-

SLIM FINDS ME ATOP THE CLIMBING WALL AN hour later. "Heard about your little threat to Slaughter."

"I know. It was stupid. I shouldn't—"

"It was brave, and it was right."

My jaw drops. *Did Slim actually pay me a compliment?*

"Don't let my flattery go to your head, Kid. It *was* stupid. I only wish I could've done the same thing. I'm not brave like you. I would've just stood there and wet my pants. That guy scares the piss out of me."

"You got the better of him once."

"Only because I had to."

I shake my head, knowing he didn't have to come to my recue. "You don't see it, but you're the bravest man I know."

Slim's cheeks turn red, and he suddenly takes an interest in his feet. I smile, recognizing his other quality: humility. He truly has the skills of a born leader. I wish more than anything that my father could've met him.

The sound of breathing pulls my focus from Slim onto the brown-skinned man climbing the wall. My stomach clenches. I'd been avoiding this conversation for a long time, but I knew I couldn't keep it away forever. I'd given Bear a lot of thought during my archery training. I wasn't sure I was ready to blame cancer for taking my mom. It was easier to blame him.

"You're starting to get a reputation as one tough shank, you know that?" Bear says, pulling himself up onto the platform.

I shrug. "Is that a bad thing?"

"Yes and no. It all depends on who you ask. Some don't like that you've become the Arena's poster boy. It may not look like it, but there is a pecking order, even in here. Some might think they can climb the ranks by taking you out."

"What he said to Slaughter was the right thing," Slim says.

"I'm not saying it wasn't. What I am saying is to take it easy. I also heard about that archer from Section Three you about knocked over."

Slim slaps my leg. "What did you do?"

"I didn't do anything! The guy was blowing kisses at me."

Bear shakes his head. "Then blow one back and get your eyes back on the target. Don't go picking fights. I heard him blabbing his mouth off to some other guys in his section about getting rid of you. You need to be careful. Those guys in Section Three are unpredictable. They're the ones that started that fiasco in the cafeteria."

"I don't like working with the other sections," Slim says. "It's hard enough to create unity in our own."

"We do what we have to." Bear's tone says he doesn't want to argue about it—and he's right. We're stuck working with them. I guess Bear could have just assigned each section to a galley, but that would be complete chaos.

"I've finally gotten the hang of the bow," I say, trying to find a new topic of conversation.

Bear gives a half grin. "That's the first thing you've said today I like." He reaches behind his back and tosses something at me. "Here." I catch the apple, look down at it, then meet his eyes. I can see regret in them, and it's like a knife to my heart. I know he's done nothing wrong. I have to let it go.

"I know it wasn't your fault." My voice sounds pathetic, more of a croak than anything. "I'm sorry for what I said."

Silence hangs in the air between us as I wait for him to accept my apology. I want him to be my friend again. I need him to be. He nods.

"I owe you an apology, too. Not for not saving your mother. I had no control over that, but for not being more forward with you about it. And I shouldn't have treated you the way I did when you entered the Arena. You see … I have a boy who's the same age as you. God knows how much I miss that kid; him and his mom. I blamed you for taking them from me. That wasn't right. It wasn't your fault I ended up in this sorry place and became what I did."

All I can do is nod in acceptance. He had a son the same age as me—a son that lost his father the day I lost my mom. It all seemed so twisted and wrong that two families were broken that day when it should only have been mine. Guilt fills me as if I'm somehow responsible for ordering his arrest. Days ago, when he told me what happened, I was ready to be his judge and jury. I wanted him to suffer the way I'd suffered. Now, I know he's been suffering all along.

"What's his name?"

"Malcolm," he says softly. "Malcolm Otis. You remind me of him, some. I imagine he's just about as tall as you, and God knows he's smart. He's probably the top of his class and on his way to making a difference in the world. At least, I hope so."

I can see the longing in his eyes. The longing I feel to be with those I love. I can't wait to hold Mary again, to feel her warm lips against mine. We have to get out of this place. Somehow, we have to set everything right.

"This plan for escape will work, right?"

Both Bear and Slim look at me, doubt written all over their faces.

"It's a risk," Bear says.

"One we're willing to take and die for," Slim adds.

I nod. I won't be waiting for the lottery to call my name, for some chance that Gerard set the whole thing up to save me. I'll be outside the Arena. I'll save myself. "What do I need to do?"

Bear exchanges a glance with Slim, then turns to me. "I need you to get your archery perfected. I've assigned you near me and Slim on the same galley. Slim will be manning a cannon. We'll use that to find our door."

"Door?" I ask, a little confused. *How could a cannon find a door?*

Slim leans forward. "You know how I was a little late getting back at the end of the group battle and you thought I was dead? Well, I was actually doing some snooping. When I fell in the river I got sucked into the tube that winds around the battlefield. A little ways into the tunnel I found a—"

"Hatch!"

Both men look at me with shocked expressions.

"I found it, too."

Slim slaps my leg again. "Well don't be so shy in saying when you find a door out of here."

"I'm sorry. I was going to, but then things got crazy and—"

"Forget it," Bear says. "We've all held things back."

I shake my head. "It doesn't matter, anyway. When we were working maintenance, I checked sector fifty and found where the hatch comes out. Besides leading to the underbelly, the only other door there is locked, and you have to have a passkey to open it."

Slim smiles at Bear. "Is this kid unreal or what? He's full of nothing but lies. He says he's working his tail off checking the pipe work and he's nosing around up ladders."

"I couldn't help it. I saw the sector and remembered the number on the wall before entering the tunnel. I had to see if it was a way out."

"It's not the way out," Bear says. "At least not the way we'll be taking. Not the door anyway. That door only leads to another level and too many locked doors to get past. Yes, we'll use the hatch, but to take us back to the underbelly."

"But there's no way out from there," I argue.

Slim smirks. "He thinks he knows everything."

"Then tell me what I don't know."

Bear pulls out his tablet and pats the cover. "Slim discovered the same as you with the door, so we thought of a new angle—but in order for it to work, I needed a map of the building."

"That head guard owed Bear a favor," Slim added. "He made it rich off Bear during a bid on a beast fight."

I couldn't believe it. "That was all rigged? The guards being there, the fight, the tablet?"

"Bear's smart, Kid."

"Wouldn't they have suspected something about escaping?"

Bear shakes his head. "I don't think so. Aside from a few things, this tablet is no different from the one they issue to each section. It helps me report our labor tasks, and it gives me assignments with fights. Because it was registered to a guard, some of the firewalls were down. I was able to retrieve a map of the colosseum's duct work."

Bear shows me a complicated maze of tunnels outlining the colosseum on the tablet's screen. I try to follow the path leading from the underbelly to an exit, but get lost.

"Wait a minute," I say. "Can't the game master see that you have that on your tablet?"

"Not anymore," Slim puts in. "To them it's just another picture of the galleys. A little trick I learned while hotwiring computer systems back in the day."

"That's ingenious! So we take the hatch to the underbelly, then somehow get up into the duct work?"

"That's what Bear and I were doing back at sector seventeen. We made sure we had everything there and ready for us. Once we make it into the duct work, we move up to the patron levels. We find a couple bozos and steal the clothes off them."

"Then what?"

"We hightail it to freedom, Kid."

I shake my head. "But how? Where do we go from there?"

Slim sighs and looks at Bear, who hesitates for a second. "We head for the outlands."

"Beyond the border? There's radiation and sickness and—"

"Freedom," Bear says. "Beyond the border is freedom. Once we're out, we'll start talking about a way to get you pardoned. Your trial was all wrong, and half this country knows it. First we have to get you out of this death trap."

"You don't know what it's like over the border wall. It could be even worse there. And how do we get past the Death Strip? We could die and never make it back to do anything."

"Better die on our own terms than stay in here," Slim argues. "Cal, I hate to burst your bubble, but someone wants you dead, and if you stay in here, sooner or later they're going to get their wish. So what, we're going out of Primus? That's not the worst thing that could happen to a person. Besides, it might be just as nice over there as it is here."

"I doubt that."

"Hey," Slim snaps. "It's freedom. I don't care if that land is filled with hot sand and nothing else, I will die a happy man, knowing I'm free."

When I thought of being free from the Arena, I thought I would be returning to my home. How naïve was I to think that? Even if I'm somehow pardoned for my crime, I won't go back to living in a mansion next to Senate Hall. I wouldn't have servants and cooks to wait on me and feed me. I'm no longer the son of a senator. That life is over. If I want freedom, I have to take what's offered to me.

But going beyond the border wall might be a death sentence all on its own. Nobody really knows what's beyond the Field; the world was at war when it went up. I was told those who tried to leave never came back. And I don't know if I want freedom if it means I'll never see Mary again. *If I go through with this, will our future hold anything more than memories?*

"Cal," Bear says, placing a hand on my shoulder. "I promise you I will do everything in my power to get your name cleared. But I need to know that you're in this one hundred percent. It's not going to be easy. Gaining freedom never has been."

My heart squeezes as the truth settles in it. I know this is my only way out. I meet Bear's eyes, then Slim's, and nod.

-TWENTY-THREE-

THE MORNING BELL BLARES, ADDING MORE pressure to my already growing headache. I sit up, stretching the aches out of my shoulders and back. I don't know how much sleep I got last night, but I know it's not enough. I need to be clear-minded, focused. Slim's snoring continues to fill the room with the singsong of a chainsaw. I shake his arm, and he wakes up with a jolt.

"Today's the day, sunshine," I say. "Let's go fill our brains with food."

He grunts, but gets to his feet in a flash. The deep rings under his eyes tell me he got as little sleep as I did. Worry and anticipation do nothing for you when it comes to getting a good night's sleep. A lot of things have to go perfectly today. This is it.

Anxious faces greet me as we enter the cafeteria. Anything could happen in the Arena today but one thing is certain: half these men will die. I try not to make eye contact with anyone, especially those I have come to look on as friends. I don't want to say goodbye without meaning to.

Hammer and Fist crack jokes when I sit down, but the banter is forced, almost as though they were ordered to laugh with a gun to their head.

The hot paste they call oatmeal does nothing to revive my sleepy mind. I try to follow Slim's example and shove plenty of fruits and nuts down my throat, but it's hard to be hungry when I know I'll soon be fighting for my life.

Bear sits down next to us. He sports a bandage around his left forearm. I open my mouth to ask what happened, but he winks at me before digging into his plate of gruel. Unlike us, he looks well-rested. Perhaps he's just used to the anticipation. Maybe he believes we'll succeed. As for me, I can only pray.

Prayer has been a hard thing for me, lately. Mom taught me the words to say when I was young, but they're lost with the memories of the past. I wonder if God is even there at all, and if he is, why did he put me in this place? To build strength? Learn humility? I'm sure there are better lesson plans for that. At times I think this is his punishment for me not being good enough—for not being the son my father truly deserved. Then again, perhaps when it comes to God, no questions are answered easily.

"Good morning, offenders," a cheerful voice sounds throughout the room. I look up at the monitor to see Scarlet Wild perched on a hammock hanging off a galley's railing. She is completely naked from the waist up with only a few strands of hair covering her breasts. She has no legs. Instead, she flicks a mermaid's tail in the water, swishing the colorful fins back and forth. Bubbles drift around her lazily as if she's in some kind of fantasyland. Some of the men shout hellos or other obscene things. Most are reserved and mute.

"I hope you are as excited as I am for this historic moment. So much time and expense has gone into tonight's event. Every detail has been carefully selected by this game's benefactor, Senator Javier Gerard. He wants this to be the best show the Arena has ever held. And I promise you it will be." Scarlet giggles and I can't help but think once again about the lottery. If this really is Gerard's plan to get me out of here, he's done a poor job of covering up his hand in it. Why not just get Katherine Marsh to let me go? Why all the theatrics?

"You have exactly thirty minutes to finish your meals. All offenders must then follow their section leaders to be outfitted for our naval battle. Mmm … I love a man in uniform. Any offender left in the compound will be shot on sight." She follows this up with another giddy laugh. She swishes her tail around, and frothy foam laps against the side of the galley. A large bubble drifts in front of her face and she pops it playfully with her index finger. Like with every other announcement, I'm sickened by the lack of humanity she has for these men. I doubt she's even met one of us face to face.

"Remember: victorious team members will all be entered into the lottery for the grand prize—a pardon from the senate! But this *is* a fight to the death, offenders. A team will not be considered victorious until every last life is extinguished on the opposing team. Will it be the Hawks, or the Falcons? This mermaid cannot tell, but she wishes you all the best of luck."

Scarlet dives into the water, revealing a jagged dorsal fin on her back. The screen fades to black. Silence drapes over the cafeteria like a thick wool blanket. No one moves. The screen lights up with the countdown and men move into action.

"Go to the rec room and get suited up," Bear orders me and Slim. "I'll meet you in the weapons vault in twenty."

Confused, I follow Slim and the crowd to the rec room where we discover stacks of brown and green fur-lined clothing lining the walls. I exchange a glance with Slim and grab a stack. In the corner of the room, next to the climbing wall, we stop to dress. Slim pulls off his gray clothes and squeezes into a pair of brown pants that balloon out in the legs.

"These look freakin' ridiculous!" he says, unsuccessfully trying to cinch the fly together. "Whoever picked out these shankin' clothes should die wearing them."

I can't help but laugh. Slim shoots me an angry glare that could melt plastic, but I ignore him and head back to the stacks of strange clothes to find him a larger pair of pants. When I find a pair I think will work, I'm suddenly brought back to what Bear said at the beginning of the week about this battle. It's supposed to be a reenactment of the Battle of

Lepanto. I rack my brain for any mention of this historical account from my textbooks, but even though history was my best subject, I can't remember much.

I stuff Slim's pants under my arm and grab two pairs of boots trimmed in dark fur from a pile and head back to Slim. I hand him the larger clothes. He accepts them with a roll of his eyes.

"What do you know about the Battle of Lepanto?" I ask.

"The what? Do I look like a freakin' history teacher?"

I sigh and pull on my own clothes, adding layer after layer—first the balloon pants followed by a long shirt and a fur-lined robe over that. I top it off with some decorative draped tunic and I'm still left with a weird bundle of fabric in my hands. I dart a glance to the other men and see some of them wrapping the fabric around their head like a headpiece. The clothes are a strange fit, hanging on me like an elaborate curtain. Something about them nags at me, but I can't quite put a finger on it. I pull up my leather boots, silently thanking the game masters for providing socks. Once I'm done, I try again with Slim.

"Have the group battles ever been fixed?"

Slim fumbles with his headpiece. "What do you mean, fixed?"

I lower my voice. "As in *fixed.* You said most of them are historical reenactments. Do the game masters ever fix the battle so the army that lost in history loses in the reenactment?"

"Kid, I don't have time to think out that shank. I have enough to worry about with remembering my attack plans, not to mention getting these bozos to follow orders." He looks up at the monitor, and I follow his stare. It's time to meet Bear in the weapons vault. Everything is happening too fast. If they'd just give me a few minutes to think, I could figure out what's bothering me.

"Come on, Kid, you look great—like a damn fool."

We head through the training room toward the vaults, and some of the offenders follow. We look like a group of strange men from an ancient land. Who wears these kinds of clothes? There's definitely more fabric than necessary. No doubt we'll shed most of it once the battle starts, especially the oarsmen. I couldn't imagine rowing a boat in all this clothing.

We find Bear leaning against the wall next to the vault. He looks like a warrior pulled straight from a history textbook. His dark brown skin is highlighted by the tan fur lining his green tunic. The fabric-wrapped hat atop his head makes him look mysterious and wise. Slim obviously think he looks as ridiculous as the rest of us and barks out a laugh.

"I guess you hoped we'd be the Spanish?" Bear asks.

The Spanish! That was it. The Battle of Lepanto was one of the last naval battles featuring galley ships. It was a battle between Spain, led by the famous Don Juan of Austria, and the Ottoman Turks. These clothes obviously aren't what the Spanish soldiers wore—our team's the Turks!

Dread fills my stomach. "Bear, we have a problem," I whisper.

He looks at me with questioning eyes, but the men behind me move in closer. If there's a problem, they want to hear it. What if what I have to say turns out not to be true? I could be filling these men's minds with negative thoughts—thoughts that won't help our situation.

"We all look like idiots," I say.

The men around us laugh. Slim's eyes move from me to Bear, and they exchange a knowing glance before joining in the laughter. Hopefully I can get them alone and explain. If this is a reenactment, and the game masters fix the battle to be historically correct, then the Hawk team is dead. The Turks lost the Battle of Lepanto. Which means every last one of us will be slaughtered. It also means that Gerard wasn't trying to get me out. The lottery isn't for me. Slim had to be right—Gerard killed my father.

Bear punches in the code on the keypad and the door to the weapons vault opens. He steps forward and the men around us gasp. There are no weapons. The room is completely empty.

"What are we supposed to fight with?" one offender shouts.

"You said we'd have knives and swords. There's nothing! You can't expect me to fight with an oar!"

The men shout curses while those in the back push forward to get a better look. The men at the front push back and suddenly fists fly. Bear shouts to the men, but I can't make out his words. I'm pushed to the back and fall onto a man who punches me in the gut. I hunch forward and suddenly I'm being trampled. I feel the soles of boots smashing my arms, legs, and head. I try to get up, but my face is met with a blast of pain. Bright stars fill my vision and everything goes black.

"YOU NEED TO WAKE UP. I CAN'T KEEP CARRYING you." I hear Bear, but it's like he's down a tunnel. His voice is muffled and echoes. My head pounds, but the pain doesn't compare with that in my left forearm. It feels like I have a knife lodged in it. I moan as he sets me on my feet. It takes me a second, but I find my balance and try to open my eyes.

Everything is blurry at first, but then I see Bear's face under that strange roll of fabric. Something glints in his hand. *A knife?* It stabs into me and I try to pull out of his grip

"Stop it," he orders. "Relax your arm."

I shake my head, but give in. "What did you do?"

"I just gave you an injection of nanorobotics. You need to walk with me now. Can you do that?"

I nod, and wish I hadn't. My head spins and I almost fall into Bear.

"Kid, you have to get it together. This is it. We've got to get to the top of the platform now, before the trumpet sounds."

Trumpet, what trumpet? I have no idea what he's talking about. No, wait. The trumpet … the naval battle. Suddenly Scarlet Wild's warning slips into my mind. *Any offender left in the compound will be shot on sight.* I force myself to move.

"What happened?"

"The damn idiots started freaking out because they cleared out the weapons vault. I tried to explain they moved them to the mirror chamber, but they wouldn't listen. We lost a couple men because of that shank."

"My arm feels broken," I whine, cupping the fabric bandaging it. We climb onto the lift and slowly begin to rise.

Bear pulls me in close, whispering in my ear. "It's not broken. I used the chaos to remove your tracker. Don't pull off that bandage until I tell you. As long as it's technically attached to you, the game masters will think you're alive. The nanos will help you recover. Don't ask what I had to do to get it. I removed my tracker last night." He nods to a bandage on his forearm.

"What about Slim?"

"I'll take care of his soon. He had to move ahead of us to organize the team onto their assigned ships. We have to be careful. I don't want the game masters to get suspicious."

"I wanted to tell you earlier about the naval battle. If they fix it—"

"I know. The Turks didn't win the battle. Unless they decide to alter the course of history, our group is as good as dead."

This knowledge is like another slug to the stomach. I hate being right sometimes. Everyone in Sections One through Three will be dead by the end of today. I try not to think about Hammer and Fist. I can't stand the thought of them dying just to appease the inhuman history buffs. Maybe we should tell them about our escape plan. Maybe we can get them out, too. The thought brings hope, even though I know it's impossible.

"So they *do* fix the battles," I mumble.

"All the time. Everything in this place is what *they* want. You survived the saber-tooth because *they* wanted you to. You said they injected you with nanorobotics. They probably gave you something when you fought that death worm. I'm not one hundred percent sure they had planned on you and Slim stealing that Eagle by climbing Slaughter's fortress. Then again, if they wanted to, they could have stopped you."

Everything he said, I'd already suspected. I'd wondered myself how I survived that death worm with nothing but toilet water to sustain me for two weeks. The game masters probably enjoyed living up to their name—constantly playing and toying with our minds. Even now, this was just a game to them. We were toy soldiers going off to war, one we wouldn't come back from.

My thoughts turn to Senator Gerard, the generous sponsor of today's bloodbath. "He wants me dead—Gerard. You heard Scarlet. He's orchestrated this whole thing. If he wanted to save me he could have made us the Spanish.

Instead he made us the freakin' Turks. He's killing our sections just to get rid of me."

Bear doesn't say anything, only looks at me with his brown eyes as we climb higher. It's as though he's known the truth about Gerard all along. Both he and Slim told me to think on it but I couldn't bring myself to think the man who I'd seen as an uncle would do this to me. I wish I knew why. Perhaps with me out of the way, there'd be no one to accuse him of my father's murder. There'd be no reason for anyone to pursue the case at all. If I don't escape, my life is over, and he'll continue to help lead Primus into a world of lies and treason.

The platform slows to a stop and my pain is forgotten as fear takes its place. My heart thumps hard in my chest as I take in my surroundings. We're on a narrow dock connecting the Hawks' six galley ships. Beyond us, a massive expanse of ocean surrounds us. I marvel that the colosseum could hold so much water, then remember it's all an illusion. For all I know, the water is only deep enough to hold the boats and only extends as far as the furthest boat. The game masters control what we see. I search across the water into the eerie fog. I don't see the enemy ships, but I know they're out there.

The galleys each have a mast, but there's no sail. Our only propulsion will be by the strength of our oarsmen. I spot Slim standing next to the cannons in the bow of the last ship. He's ditched his fabric hat and tunic and is shouting orders to Hammer and Fist, who have command of the galleys next to him. Bear rushes up the plank leading from the dock to Slim's ship and I follow. The second my boot touches the deck, a trumpet blares, filling the Arena. The spectators' cheers are so loud they drown out the trumpet, and I wonder how many people are watching from the stands. This has to be the most costly and desirable battle in the Arena's history. How much are the citizens of Primus willing to pay to see so many men die?

Only a small boardwalk separates the oarsmen on either side of the ship, and it's crowded with fighters. I spot two archers at the rear of the ship but follow behind Bear instead of taking my place with them. I weave my way through the crowd of men, trying not to trip. I glance at their faces, wondering if any of them was the one who slugged me in the gut back in the compound. I guess it doesn't matter.

The slap of water fills the air as the oarsmen begin to heave themselves back and forth, moving us away from the dock. I climb the five steps to the platform, eyeing the crates of cannonballs and barrels of powder under the steps.

By the time I reach Slim, my heart is racing and my hands are sweaty. He hands me a bow, a fat quiver full of arrows, and three provision sacks. "Since you decided to take a nap, I got your stuff."

"Thanks," I say, noticing three more provision sacks slung over his shoulder. I think his obsession with food has gone too far—then I realize the provisions aren't just for this battle. They're for after, when we escape. We are heading to the wastelands beyond the border, and we'll need food.

Slim smiles and nods, then pulls me close for a rough hug. "The second you see an opportunity to get a knife, do it. They're pretty handy, if you catch my drift."

I nod, afraid if I speak, nothing but the squeak of a mouse will come out. Slim and Bear have planned everything. I just hope it all works out.

"Now, find a spot up there and do some lookout work." Slim points to the top of the mast where a small barrel rests on a tiny platform—he calls it the crow's nest. He's got to be freaking crazy! I start to complain, but his brow lowers and he shakes his head. He means business, and there's no room to argue. I move toward the mast, but Bear beats me to it.

He climbs the mast until he reaches the long beam where a sail would normally be tied. He lifts himself onto the beam, then stands and looks downward on us. He pulls a curved sword from the sheath at his waist and holds it toward the artificial sky. His baritone voice is like a cannon boom.

"Row, men, row! Row as you have never done before. Today we change the history books. Today we give these people a fight unlike the one they read about. Row! Row! Row!"

The men sound a war cry, the audience cheers. A man at the back of the ship begins to hammer on a drum and the oarsmen paddle with the beat. Our galley moves forward alongside the line of ancient ships. Bear lifts his sword even higher and his voice calls out over the cacophony of noise as if he's the angel of death.

"You will not have us! We defy you! We are men! We have come to win … for Malcolm!"

"For my mama!" Slim cries.

I lift my bow and join the call. "For Mary!"

-TWENTY-FOUR-

WE LEAD THE HAWKS IN V-FORMATION WITH Hammer and Fist flanking our sides. The rolling fog is anything but helpful. I see phantom ships here and there, but it could just be my imagination, or tricks from the game masters—a diversion from the real threat which could be somewhere else. Waves hit the side of the galley, rocking me back and forth. I try not to think about how sick the motion makes me.

Bear now stands on deck, keeping a watchful eye, like me, on the churning waves. I'd rather be down there with him and Slim. The crow's nest is claustrophobic, nauseating, and annoying. The flag, embossed with a golden silhouette of a Hawk, whips and flaps in the wind, sometimes striking me in the face. Maybe I'm up here because Bear wants me away from the action, but I feel disconnected from the men below.

"Ready the cannons!" Bear shouts over the beating drum and the huffing and puffing of the oarsmen.

Hammer and Fist echo the order, and I assume the other three galley captains do likewise, but they're too far away for

me to hear. Slim and two other men pack one of the long barrels with a charge of gunpowder, then load it with a fat lead ball. I pull my eyes from their work and back to my job as lookout, staring out into the drifting fog, waiting, waiting for any sign of the Falcon ships. With Bear's order, I half expect to see them in front of us, but still there's nothing but tumbling fog.

Where are they? I dare a glance back toward the docks to see if I can determine how far we've gone, when something flickers in the murkiness. Cold icy fear ripples up my back.

"Bear! They're behind us! Behind us!"

Boom—ba—boom—boom!

Four Falcon galleys emerge from the fog like ghost ships. They attack with vengeance, their cannonballs ripping apart our galleys closest to them. Bear screams for us to turn about. The drummer slams on his drum, increasing the rhythm. The oarsmen grunt in reply, and my stomach does a flip-flop with the sudden change in direction. The Falcon galleys reach our furthest ship. They close in so fast, it's as though they're equipped with motors. The spectators' cheers mix with the sound of metal on metal. *Where are their other two ships?*

Ba—boom!

I'm thrown forward, my shoulder smacking hard into the mast. *Hit! We've been hit!* An angry billow of smoke clouds my vision of the deck below. I hear Bear shouting orders, but I can't make out the words over the ringing in my ears.

Boom!

Water rains down on my face. I wipe it away and see the other two Falcon ships cutting through the fog toward us. "To the left!" My voice sounds distant, but I'm screaming as loud as I can. "Two galleys coming at us from the left! Bear, the left!"

I lurch to the side as our galley shifts toward the rival ships. The smoke settles, and I see where the first ball hit, removing some of the beautifully carved cherubim framing the stern. A few men are injured. This hit has only fueled our team's anger. They raise their fists and blades, shouting curses at the sky. Another cannonball hits the water next to us, blasting a spray up and over the sides of the deck, drenching the oarsmen.

"Now!" Slim orders. I feel a vibration rock up the mast as our cannons fire. Both balls miss their targets, and Slim shouts a curse, then orders the men to reload. The men clean the barrels and begin packing down the charge. *Slow. Too slow.*

Ba—boom! Boom!

Hammer and Fist fire, each making a direct hit on the closest of the Falcon's galleys. The crowd erupts in loud applause.

"Row, men! Row!" Bear calls. The drummer picks up the beat and the oarsmen scream their reply. I can only imagine how their muscles must feel. We move in closer and closer to the Falcon's lead ship. Slim fires again, and I'm rocked back with the vibration. This time both balls find their mark, and the Falcon's front galley explodes in a ball of flame.

Offenders dressed in red, white and yellow uniforms leap from the ship, abandoning it to the flames. Our men cheer along with the spectators.

Hammer and Fist close in on the second Falcon galley, trapping it between them, as Bear orders us toward the wrecked ship. The closer we get, the louder the screams become. The men in the water thrash about, trying to climb back onto the burning ship as though they've jumped into boiling water.

Something else catches my eye—a gray dorsal fin cuts through the debris-filled water just a few yards in front of us, heading toward the wreck. I spot another, and another. One of the men is halfway up the side of the galley when a great white shark bursts from the water, taking the man's legs in its jaws. Blood tints the water red as the man cries out one last time before being pulled down.

The crowd of spectators celebrates this new twist to our naval battle with whoops and shouts of jubilation—it sickens me. The sharks are in a blood frenzy as they tear and snap at anything that moves. A shout from below draws my focus from the wreck. An oarsman is struggling with his paddle that's clamped in the jaws of another great white. The strength of the shark nearly lifts the man up out of his seat. The archers on deck let their arrows fly, and finally the shark disappears beneath the churning waves.

"Get us out of here!" Bear orders.

The oarsmen set to work, and we move away from the wreck. Injured men call out, pleading for us to come back, but we don't. This is a fight to the death. There's no room to do the right thing.

Bear and Slim look up at me, concern in their eyes. I know what they're thinking—for our plan to work, we have to find the tunnel's entrance under water. We never imagined there'd be sharks.

More booms sound. Hammer has closed in on the Falcons and is preparing to board; Fist's ship is just behind. Bear orders us to meet them and I search for our other ships, but see nothing through the fog that's rolled in again. Cannon fire continues, but the blasts are now few and far between. My eyes return to Hammer and Fist. They each storm their respective galleys, throwing men into the water and killing others with swords. It doesn't take long for the shark fins to reappear.

Our archers shoot at the water, finding the sharks a common enemy. I want to help, but I can barely move in this nest, let alone loose an arrow. I pull myself out of the barrel and straddle the mast before finding the first rung of the ladder with my boot. I don't care what Bear says, I can't just sit up here and watch men die.

Boom!

I'm thrown back, flipping head over heels before plunging into the frigid water.

I remember watching a pre-atomic wars documentary on great white sharks in school and how I felt at seeing the great predator of the oceans. I was both mesmerized and terrified.

They were strong, fast, and relentless—no doubt the game masters created this breed to be the same. Any minute they'll find me, bite me, rip me apart.

My lungs burn with the need to breathe. I kick as hard as I can, feeling the weight of my bow, quiver, provisions sacks, and all the fabric holding me down. Finally, I break the surface and suck in a breath, only to have it forced out of me with a blow to my back.

I surface again, finding myself struggling with an oar. I grab hold, but am quickly beaten off by another. I try to shout, but the oarsman can't hear me—I doubt anyone can see me. I take one last breath and dive back down. Ignoring the sting in my eyes from the salt water, I search for a safe place to surface. There, a few yards away, the water's surface is clear of the constant dip and swing of the oars. I swim as hard as I can, struggling against the burdens that weigh me down. I'm just a few feet away when I see it—a shark.

-TWENTY-FIVE-

I'VE FACED DEATH SO OFTEN IN THE ARENA, I feel almost used to it. The way time slows, the rhythmic pounding of my heart, the rush-rush of blood in my ears—it's all familiar. This death is not in the form of an ancient cat, or some mythical death worm, or even the scarred face of an inmate. No matter what mask death decides to wear, it always feels the same. Hopeless, utterly hopeless.

I wonder if I'll drown before the shark reaches me. I wonder how fast it can swim—and my mind is overwhelmed with useless facts I learned in school. How the great white weighs over fifteen hundred pounds, how it has three hundred teeth arranged in several rows, how its bite is twenty times stronger than that of a human. I want to think about other things. I don't want fear of this predator to be the last thought in my mind before I die.

I close my eyes and search for a memory of Mary. It comes easily. I see her standing under the apple tree in the school yard, her honey-colored hair blowing gently in the breeze, her lips, soft as rose petals, curved upwards in a delicious grin. I think of her voice, and my fears wash away. My heart slows and the sound of rushing blood in my ears fades. This death is different. It's almost sweet, almost peaceful. I open my eyes, prepared to accept what comes.

The shark is gone.

I see nothing but an ocean of water. I don't hesitate. I swim upward, and my head breaks the surface. I pull the precious air into my lungs, confused at my luck yet grateful the shark found better prey.

The sound of fighting pulls me around. One of the Falcon ships must have rammed our galley. The ship's stern is on fire, and the mast that once held my perch is gone. Oarsmen are now fighting, some using their oars as weapons, some using blades. I search the mass of men, trying to find Bear and Slim.

I spot Bear fighting with a group of oarsmen, but can't find Slim. I want to head back to help my teammates, but I can see the shark fins circling the galleys. I don't want to add my own body to the carnage. Bear cuts a way back to the stern, motioning with his hands for the men to put out the fire. Several men begin beating the flames with their wet turbans as Bear moves on to taking back control of the galley.

A sudden blast from the cannons draws my attention to the bow of the ship. I finally see Slim—he's just fired a cannonball out to sea where there's nothing in sight. He loads the other cannon and fires again. The cannonball flies off into oblivion and suddenly explodes.

The rolling fog and waves flicker and vanish.

I'm not swimming in the ocean, but a large cement bowl filled with water. I look up and, for the first time, I can see the colosseum for what it truly is—nothing more than a sports arena. There are rows upon rows of shouting, waving spectators in at least twenty levels of stadium seats. Flashes from hovercams twinkle here and there. Jumbo screens with zoomed in footage of the naval battle hover in the center of what appears to be a night sky beyond the open-air structure. The view flickers in and out as the game masters work to hide them from us.

A monotone voice blares out, telling the crowd to remain calm and no one will be hurt. I almost laugh at the statement. Down here, plenty of men are being hurt. Reality flickers in and out. I quickly scan the wall, searching for the section numbers. Just before the fog and ocean return, I see it—sector fifty.

I won't escape without Bear and Slim, but I can't just sit here and wait to see what happens next. I do the only thing I can think of: I kill myself.

With the bandage and tracker removed, it should tell the game masters that I've met my end. I'm not sure if this is when Bear would have me do it or not, but I can't risk anyone monitoring my tracker seeing me move toward the emergency exit. Let them think a shark got me. Perhaps they got good footage of me falling into the water. A small pang of guilt strikes me, knowing that Mary is probably watching at home. Would they announce my death right away? How will she take losing me again, really losing me?

The hope of maybe one day being with her renews my energy. I swim as hard and as fast as I can, mentally keeping an image in my mind of where the number fifty was printed on the wall. I don't think about sharks, I don't think about the galleys, or who will win this horrible battle. I only think of Mary and how it will be to hold her in my arms and tell her I didn't really die here.

I look up and the rolling fog shimmers out of focus. I'm close to the wall. I'm almost there. I dive down and search for the tunnel. I don't find it on my first dive, but my second. It's further down than I thought it would be and completely filled with water. The disappointment is like a punch to the gut. I've gotten here, but there's no way to move forward. No way to escape.

Something brushes past my back and all my muscles tense. I kick to the surface and turn around, expecting to see the dorsal fin of a shark, when I'm greeted with Bear's brown face. Behind him, Slim treads water.

"Kid, you surprise me every day," Bear says between panting breaths. "I almost thought we'd lost you."

"Me, surprise you? You guys nearly made me piss my pants."

Slim laughs and moves in closer. His face is red and he's breathing even harder than Bear. It's time to tell them the bad news. "The tunnel's too far down and filled with water. We won't be able to breathe."

Slim rolls his eyes. "Don't you ever freakin' use your head, Kid? You've got two perfectly good airbags right on ya."

"Take off your boots," Bear says. "We'll fill them with air and use them to breathe."

"That will work?"

Bear shrugs. "Theoretically, yes."

"I think it all depends on how bad your boot smells, personally," Slim jokes. I force a laugh, then do my best to pull off my boots, getting plenty of water up my nose in the process. Once they're off, I follow Slim as he flips a boot over and slowly lowers it under the water with the sole pointing straight up. I notice his forearm is bleeding and wonder how on earth Bear found the time during all the fighting to remove Slim's tracker without anyone noticing.

Slim catches my eye. "You got rid of your tracker, right?"

"Right after you showed me the way to go."

"Good boy."

"Only breathe in if you absolutely have to," Bear warns. "I'm not sure how long it will take us to open the hatch. Let's get out of here before someone gets bored watching the fight and spots us. You ready?"

I nod. There's no going back now. We either escape, or we die trying.

Bear dives down. I breathe in and out then suck in a deep gulp of air before following. I watch Bear as he uses his head and shoulders to navigate. I try to do the same. I have to keep reminding myself not to move my arms. I don't want to lose the air in my boots. Already, I can see tiny bubbles spilling out from around the soles. Hopefully there'll be air left in them when I need it. We're just a few feet from the tunnel's entrance when something out of the corner of my eye makes me flinch.

A shark moves through the water toward us. Bear doesn't notice as he continues toward the tunnel. I look back to Slim and see a trail of red snaking its way from the wound on his arm. This is not good.

I motion with my leg for Slim to hurry. He shakes his head, not getting my message. I do it again, pointing the best I can with my sock-foot. Finally he looks to his right and sees the shark.

Terror breaks over his face and suddenly the blood trail from his arm is thicker. The shark comes in fast, circling through the stream of blood. Human remains cling to its teeth, and it snaps its powerful jaws. The predator can't possibly be hungry, yet it looks ready to try another course—probably programed that way.

It takes too long to reach Bear at the tunnel. His eyes bulge as he comprehends our problem. He disappears into the tunnel, then returns with a long knife in hand. First I worry about where his boots are, then I worry about getting past Bear and into the tunnel without getting cut. I do my best to maneuver around him and head straight into the tunnel.

Bear's boots rest atop the tunnel's ceiling, the air holding them in place. I set mine next to his and return to the entrance. The shark closes in on Slim. He panics as one of his boots flips over. He grabs it, but loses the air in his other. He leaves the boots and swims toward us. Bear stands like a warrior, holding one hand to the tunnel, the other ready to take on the great white with just a knife. The thought is ridiculous—mine is even worse.

I pull the bow over my shoulder and nock an arrow. I pull the bowstring back and take aim. I have no idea if it's even possible to release an arrow under water, but I have to try something. Bear pulls Slim into the tunnel as the shark opens its mouth, exposing its sharp, jagged teeth. Slim's leg is too close. I release the arrow and it slices through the water, striking the shark directly in the throat. The shark shakes wildly, then races off. I float back against the tunnel wall and release what's left in my lungs.

Slim is safe. We are safe. For now.

Slim takes a drag from Bear's extra boot and I can almost hear the unsaid joke about it smelling bad. Bear retrieves one of my boots and shows me how to breathe. I'm hesitant to try. What if there's no air in it? I'll just be sucking in water. Nervously, I lift my face to the boot's opening and try to test it, flicking my tongue around, feeling for water but finding none that I can tell. Bracing myself, I breathe in. It's air—glorious air.

We swim, making our way to the emergency exit. I have to breathe two more times before we reach it. Bear and Slim turn the large wheel. Huge bubbles of air burst into the tunnel and Bear quickly grabs me, shoving me through the door. I fall onto the platform. I breathe in so much air it almost makes me dizzy. Water rushes in from the doorway, spilling down the shaft. Bear and Slim pull it closed but struggle to turn the wheel. It takes what feels like forever until the rush of water is gone, leaving only the sound of panting men.

Bear gives us only a few minutes to catch our breath. In that time we ditch the cumbersome clothing, leaving just our shirts, pants, and boots before he pushes us to move down the long ladder to the catwalk. I'm grateful for the boots. My feet remember how uncomfortable walking along the grated platform was. I look down and see the cement floor below covered in water. Will it give us away? Maybe they'll think one of the pipes leaked. Thinking about a leak makes me nervous—above us, the stadium is filled with thousands of gallons of water and people. I don't like the idea of being beneath it all if it came crashing down.

Bear is fast on his feet and impossibly quiet. I try to do the same, but clank and swish each time I step down. My heart races the further we move down the catwalk. Yes, we get closer to freedom, but we also have a higher chance at getting caught. They'll probably shoot us on sight if we're spotted. I doubt they'd just throw us back in the battle. Then again, Katherine Marsh is sadistic. She'd probably come up with a punishment even greater than death.

We make it to sector seventeen, and Bear pulls out a tool

bag stashed up in the pipe work. He rummages in the bag and hands us each a socket wrench. Slim immediately sets to work on a steel sheet covering one of the large ducts, turning the fat bolts and catching them as they fall. I do the same. In no time the cover is off, revealing a long wide shaft that goes nowhere but up.

"You're up, Kid," Slim says in a whisper.

"What am I doing?"

Slim tugs on the bowstring across my chest. At the same time, Bear pulls one of the arrows from my quiver, clamps a thin metal loop with some pliers, then attaches a metal wire. "This wire will only hold one of us at a time," Bear says. "It will take time, but we'll all make it."

Slim points a flashlight he'd taken from the tool bag up the shaft. "See where the duct turns? You need to shoot the arrow through that and then pull back on the line as soon as it goes through. Then we climb."

"I'm not sure I can hit that. I haven't been practicing shooting up, only across. Why don't you do it?"

Slim holds up his arm. He wrapped it, but it's still bleeding. "If I were right-handed, it wouldn't be a problem."

"This is why you guys forced me to learn archery?" They both nod, and I fight to hold back the anger. How can they put everything on me? What if I miss? What if I make too much noise and alert the guards? Why are they putting this much faith in a skill I didn't have a few days ago?

"Cal, you can do this," Bear says. "You just need to try."

I bite down on my lip, then exhale. We don't have all night. Soon the naval battle will end and the guards will have nothing to distract them. I take the arrow from Bear and nock it. I pull back and rest the bowstring next to my nose. It feels different with the loop and wire, but I try to ignore them. I look up at the shaft and picture a target at the end. I mentally count to three and release.

-TWENTY-SIX-

CLIMBING THE WIRE IS HARD, BUT THE JOY AT finding my target keeps me going. Even with my hands wrapped in fabric, I still feel it cutting into my skin. By the time I reach the bend in the vent, my arms, hands, and legs are shaking. I rest against the cold metal vent and call down to Slim that he can start. He mumbles something about wishing he had an ascender. I'm not sure what that is, but if it made climbing better, I wish we had one, too. I'm not sure how long it took me to climb the shaft, but it feels like forever. I wonder if the naval battle is still going, if Hammer and Fist are still alive, if by some miracle the Hawks will beat the Falcons, or if the game masters will stick with the outcome in the history books.

I lean back and close my eyes. I don't want to think about the horrors of the Arena. I push those thoughts away and focus on Mary, my beautiful, wonderful Mary. One day, I promise myself, I will see her again and it will make this all worth it. I'll smell her hair, touch her skin, breathe her air. I wish for what seems the thousandth time that I could have said goodbye to her properly—told her that I love her. If I could go back and change that one moment, I would. Oh, how I want to be back in that moment, holding her body against mine as we lie together, her whispering *I love you.*

I suddenly see my father's angry eyes glaring at her like some spoiled meat that needs tossing. It hurts me inside to know he hated her, reviled her very existence. I reach up and rub my cheek, almost recalling the sting of his slap. He was so angry, and for what? The blue brand on her arm? Senator Gerard said that Dad was in support of the end of the blue brand, yet he acted as though it was the opposite. I don't know what is true, anymore.

I never agreed with the laws set into place regarding the defectors. Before the atomic wars, plenty of countries had disagreements resulting in civil wars. Even the United States of America, Primus' forefather country, had one. The history shows that those that defected from the Union were eventually accepted back without any reservations. Doing so brought decades of prosperity to their country. Had the senate welcomed back the defectors—not made them pay for their mistakes over and over, none of this would ever have happened. Dad would've loved Mary. I would never have threatened his life and Gerard wouldn't have had me to pin his murder on. Perhaps Dad would even still be alive. I would be free, and Primus would be a peaceful nation. There's an ugly truth that history tells us, but we don't want to hear—humans never learn.

Slim's heavy breathing pulls me from my depressing thoughts, and I peek over the ledge. He's only a foot or two away. "You need a hand?"

He shakes his head. "You can barely lift yourself."

It takes a few more minutes before he's resting with me and waiting for Bear.

"Have you been eating?"

"Huh?"

"Kid, haven't you listened to a thing I've told you? You need to keep your body fueled. Open one of these bags and hand me some brain food."

I toss him a bag of nuts, and we eat. Occasionally I look down the shaft to check on Bear. He's faster than either of us, but that doesn't surprise me. The guy is tough—in many more ways than one. It takes him half the time it took me and Slim, and soon we're heading through a maze of ventilation shafts.

Occasionally I feel a blast of air that smells fresh. I breathe it in, thinking of how it came from outside the prison. It's that thought of freedom that keeps me climbing when we come to another shaft and another and another.

"How many more of these do we have?" I ask, pulling back on the bowstring. "Tell me I won't run out of arrows."

"We'll have enough," Bear says. "Just keep your hands steady."

"Easy for you to say. They're killing me."

Slim points the light up the shaft, but I can't make out

the target. The shaft just goes on and on. "It's no use. I can't see what I'm supposed to be shooting at."

"Did we turn the wrong way back there?" Slim asks Bear.

Bear shakes his head. "Couldn't have. I memorized the turns. This shaft is just a little taller than the last. Try to visualize the same striking point as the last few, and aim for that."

"You want me to visualize?" I shake my head. "That's just stupid. What if it doesn't hit?"

"Then you try again," Bear snaps. "Cal, this is our only option. We need to climb up at least one more shaft to be on the patrons' floor."

"Hey, climb on my shoulders," Slim offers.

I shake my head, knowing it won't work. "I don't think I could turn the bow enough to shoot straight up. Shine the light one more time, and I'll try to *visualize* it. But I'm not making any promises. Which way does the shaft turn up there?"

"To the left," Bear says confidently.

Slim shines the light up the shaft and I try to picture in my mind where the turn is. I pull back as hard as I can on the bowstring and the muscle in my elbow screams with discomfort. I release and hope to hit something. A second later I hear the ping-ping of the arrow as it whooshes back down. We all step out of the way.

"You hit something," Slim says, eyeing the broken arrow.

"You must have hit a bolt or something, maybe a steel converter connecting the shaft to the duct." Bear unhooks the wire from the broken arrow, connects it to a new one, and hands it to me. "Try again."

I don't argue this time. Knowing I hit something proves that I can shoot that high. It might take me a few times, but I can do this. I nock the arrow, pull back on the bow string, and release. Again the arrow falls. Again it's broken. I try two more times with the same result.

"Something's not right," Slim says. "It's like he's hitting a cement wall or something."

Bear pushes us out of the way and shines the light up the shaft. *Maybe we did take the wrong turn?* Bear tosses the flashlight to me. "Slim, climb on me. Cal, you climb up on him. Take a look up there."

Bear doesn't even make a sound as Slim lifts his heavy body atop his, reaffirming just how strong the man is. For me, it's a little more difficult to climb up two men. They're both still damp, sweaty, and smell ripe. By the time I reach Slim's shoulders, our tower shakes on Bear's trembling legs. I shine the light up the shaft and my stomach sinks. It's not a ceiling, but it might as well be. "It's a steel grate. This is a dead end."

I climb down and we all take a moment to rest and think about our next move. Slim keeps muttering under his breath while following an invisible map with his index finger in the air, as if recalculating our path through the maze. Bear sits in silence on the floor. I can see fear beginning to break through his stoic expression. This really can't be it. The ducts lead off into so many different directions, there has to be one that leads up to a higher level.

"We can't give up," I say. "Let's head back and try another vent."

"The other vents lead to fans, Kid," Slim says. "We can't stop the fans."

"What about cutting through the vent wall? You have tools. We can cut a hole and climb through. Maybe we climb on the outside of the vents instead of the inside."

Bear shakes his head. "It would take days for us to cut through this. We don't have days. Once the battle is over, they'll gather up the bodies. They won't find ours."

"They'll think we got eaten by sharks," I say.

"They count *all* the bodies," Bear says with finality.

The thought of going through the devoured remains of the offenders to count them only adds to the churning in my stomach. If Bear and Slim are giving up, then this is it. The only way forward is the way back, back to the hell of the fights and killing. *No!* We have to get out of this place. I have to try something.

I pull off my quiver, drop it next to my bow, and start pulling my feet out of my boots. I yank off my socks, thinking this will work better barefooted.

"What are you doing?" Slim asks.

"Give me the tool bag," I say, ignoring his question.

Slim doesn't ask what for, he just hands it over. I quickly pull it over my shoulder and look up at the shaft. "Bear, can you give me a boost?"

"The shaft is blocked," he grumbles.

"That doesn't mean I can't try to remove the grate. Please, Bear, I have to try something. We're not going back. I'd rather live like a rat in these vents than go back."

Bear turns away and I think he really has given up, but then he digs the coil of wire out of his bag and hands it to me. "If you can find a way to get the grate open, send us a lifeline."

I nod, and he bends down to boost me up. Once I'm in the shaft, I plant my feet hard against the wall and my back against the opposite side. Bear helps me get momentum by pushing me up into the shaft. I climb pretty fast at first, but quickly slow down. The stress on my legs is enough to make me want to quit, but the thought of freedom makes me climb higher. By the time I reach the grate, I'm covered in sweat. But it's more than exertion that has my legs and arms trembling. With fear eating at my insides, I pull out the wire, tie it around my waist, and thread it through the grate. At least if I slip, I won't fall.

The grate is attached to the side of the vent by a hinge, and sealed shut by an electronic lock. I retrieve the tools, shimmy them through the small opening in the grate, and try to cut the lock. It's too thick, and I lack the strength. "Any of you good with electronic locks?" I call down.

"A little," Slim replies.

"I'm going to drop down. Can you climb up? You'll have to brace yourself against the wall, but I've got the wire looped through the grate. You can use it as a pulley."

"Let me try," Slim says.

I hold tight to the coil of wire and slowly lower myself down the shaft. When I reach the bottom, and my legs take my weight, they give out, and I crumple. Bear helps me sit down. "You're pretty brilliant, you know that? This might actually work."

"It's up to you, Slim." I hold out the flashlight.

He nods, takes the light, and a grin lifts the corners of his lips. "And Mama said I'd never learn anything useful out on the streets. Sheesh! Come on Papa Bear, I'll need a boost, too."

"Just be careful when you short out the lock that you don't set off an alarm," Bear warns as he braces Slim's leg. "Check for extra wires."

Slim grunts a reply as he climbs into the shaft. Once he's in, Bear grabs the loose end of the wire and pulls. Slim pants loudly the whole way up, and I wonder if I sounded that bad climbing up. I use the time to get my socks and boots back on and refuel on dried meat and water—all the while sending positive thoughts up to Slim. He has to get that lock off.

"I'm … up," he calls down. "Now … I'm gunna … try."

"Don't talk," Bear orders. "Save your energy to get that damn lock off."

"Aye, aye … captain."

A good five minutes pass before I hear anything from above. Then the grate slams against the wall of the shaft and Slim shouts down a prayer of thanks to God and his mama. "Come on up, boys."

I don't hesitate. When Bear hands me the wire, I ignore the ache in my legs, and climb. We work our way through a few more turns and minor inclines before I hear the muffled sound of cheers. With them, my heart rate picks up again, thumping loud and hard in my ears.

"That sound is the call of victory," Slim whispers. "We're almost there, Kid."

We round one more corner and I see light spilling into the vent from a slatted covering. Bear and Slim hurry to clip the bolts fixing the cover to the wall. We're on the threshold of freedom. Soon, we will be rid of this nightmare and we'll be able to dream again. The sound of distant laughter and clapping filters through the vent. I can smell the sweet scents of delicious food. I can feel our independence seeping through the slats, blending with the light beyond the barrier. It's so close. All we have to do is find some clothes, blend in with the crowd, and stroll out of the Arena. This is it!

Bear removes the last bolt and we silently lift the vent from the wall. Bear nods and slowly climbs out, followed by Slim. They freeze as the red light of a hovercam fills the hall. A sudden siren fills the air and my breath catches.

"Damn it, run!" Bear shouts.

I climb out of the shaft and run, the soles of my boots slapping against the polished floor. Bear tears down the hallway, and Slim and I follow. *He's got to know where a door is!* A few people in the hall scream as we pass, shielding themselves with purses or large drinks. We just sail past them without any thought—we have to find an exit. We can't make it this far only to go back. We pass large screens here and there, showcasing the naval battle, but I don't chance a glance to see who's winning.

"This way!" Slim calls. We all turn down a long corridor and skid to a stop. A group of guards in crimson uniforms charges up the hall, mirrored masks covering their faces, batons raised in their fists. We turn. More guards move in, surrounding us. Bear and Slim pull out their knives. I unsling the bow from my shoulder, nock an arrow. I won't kill, not now, but we have to get past these men. I aim for the lead guard's legs, and shoot.

The arrow embeds just above the kneecap and the guard falls back, clearing a small gap in the line. We take it. Bear and Slim strike out at the guards, then cower back from their shining blades. We break free of their line and speed down the corridor, only to find it blocked by another line of guards. These men level guns at us, and we stop.

Slim turns to me. "I'm sorry. I must've set off an alarm with that lock."

"Forget it," I whisper. It's not his fault. We were bound to fail. This, after all, is an inescapable prison. Escape was only a dream.

The guards move in.

Bear is the first to raise his hands in surrender.

-TWENTY-SEVEN-

THE WORDS OF THE JUDGE SENTENCING ME to life in the Arena repeat over and over in my head as the guards file us into the elevator, guns pressed against our spines. How I wish I could see one of their faces. Perhaps I could try to reason with them, get someone to listen. Maybe they would believe me when I tell them I didn't kill my father, that this is just one huge mistake.

Two of the guards use their cardkeys on the panels to either side of the doorway. The doors slide shut and my stomach lurches as we move upward.

"Where are you taking us?" Bear asks.

A guard strikes him in the head with the back of his gun. "No talking."

Where are they taking us? The compound was down, not up. Moments later, the lift comes to a stop, and the doors slide open. I'm shoved forward. I can still hear the crowd cheering, but this time they're chanting something. It takes me a second, but I figure out the word they're repeating: *lottery*.

The naval battle must be over.

We're pushed toward two large double doors at the end of a long hallway. When we enter the room, I'm blown away by what I see. A long white table circles the room with several computer screens on it, manned by men and women in white uniforms. In the center of the room is a large green screen. Before it, sitting on a stage prop made to look like the bow of a ship, is none other than Scarlet Wild in her mermaid costume.

"And the winner of the lottery, who will receive a full pardon by the senate of Primus is offender—" Scarlet screams a blood curdling cry as her eyes connect with mine. The technicians around the tables lurch to their feet, then back away when they see us and our guards crowding into the room.

"Settle down, settle down!" a female voice orders. Katherine Marsh descends from a very comfortable sitting area overlooking the control room. Once again, she's wearing a crimson dress, but not her white lab coat. Behind her, I see two very familiar faces: the pudgy face of Senator Lindt, and my father's best friend, Senator Gerard.

The man I once considered an uncle looks years older than I remember. He's dressed in a tuxedo, no doubt celebrating my alleged death. *Is that shock or fear on his face?*

"We have them secured, people," Katherine says to the technicians, reaching the final step and lifting her tablet to rest in the crook of her arm. "All cameras off the offenders and back on the mermaid. Now, Scarlet, finish your statement, so you can get off that boat and get some clothes on."

Scarlet's chin quivers, and it almost makes me laugh. I doubt she's ever been in the same room as an offender, let alone three. Nervously, she turns back to the camera and Katherine motions for one of the technicians to resume recording. "I … um … the winner of the lottery, who will receive a full pardon by the senate of Primus is offender DC66, also known by many as Slaughter."

A thunderous cheer fills the stadium through the control room speakers. My heart sinks.

"You've got to be kidding me! That man's a killer and you're going to let him out?!" A guard slams me in the shoulder with the back of his gun and I fall forward.

Scarlet screams again and falls off the stage prop. She wiggles her legs free from her mermaid tail and runs to the arms of a man who covers her naked body with a purple robe.

"What in the hell is going on here?" Gerard shouts. "This boy is supposed to be dead. They're all supposed to be dead. That was the deal."

"They were caught escaping," Katherine says, her voice showing no inflection, no emotion at all. "I want them questioned before they're returned to the compound."

"Questioned! Don't question them, kill them!" Senator Lindt orders.

"Senator, I understand your concerns for them being here, but I have to know exactly how they escaped, so I can better fortify my security. I can't have offenders coming in and out of the Arena whenever they choose. I'll take care of them *after* I get what I want."

"So that's it?" I ask. A guard raises his arm to strike me again, but Katherine holds up a hand, and he backs off. "You're just going to send us back?"

"No." Katherine half-laughs. "That would be too easy. I think we can come up with a better punishment for you." She lifts her tablet and types in a few commands.

"I won't go. You can kill me right now, but I won't go back. I'm innocent. You know that. You *know* it!" I turn from Katherine and stare hard at Gerard. He avoids my eyes. Instead, he shakes his head and nervously yanks a handkerchief from his breast pocket, wiping at the perspiration on his forehead. "Why don't you tell them how you killed my father?"

"How dare you?" Gerard snaps, slamming his hands down on the railing. "I won't take any more of this, Katherine. Remove these offenders this instant, or I'm pulling my funding from this institution."

"Tell them! Tell them how you killed your best friend and framed his son for the murder."

"Shut up!"

Senator Lindt chuckles, patting his very round belly. "Calvin, you are very much wrong. I was present at your trial. I saw the footage. I'm sure everyone in this room saw the footage. You're as guilty as they come." He chuckles again and some of the technicians around the table add their laughter to his.

"Was my father for, or against, the end of the blue brand?"

Senator Lindt's bushy eyebrows lift in confusion. "What does that have to do with you killing him?"

"Answer the question," Bear booms, and even though we aren't even close to striking distance, the fat man cringes. A guard strikes Bear across the face but he stands tall. Again Katherine holds up a hand and the guard backs down.

"He was against it," Senator Lindt says. "He, like the rest of us, felt that most of our problems only occurred by allowing defectors back into society."

"Yet the senate is moving to end the blue brand?" Bear asks through gritted teeth.

"With the deaths of Sawyer, Billings, and Watson our motion was struck down. We didn't have enough votes."

Slim laughs. "A little convenient, wouldn't you say, Senator?"

"Why are you allowing them to question a senator, Katherine?" Gerard's hands are now knuckle white as he clings to the railing, fury in his eyes. "This is uncalled for. They're criminals. This is not a social club. I demand you put a stop to this, this instant!"

"Javier, there's no reason to shout," Senator Lindt says. "We have enough hysterics from that woman over there. But really, Director Marsh, enough is enough."

Katherine nods in agreement and taps a few commands into her tablet. "Scarlet, let the patrons know we have one last fight tonight."

"Waa-what?" Scarlet is taken aback and the man next to her begins touching up her smudged makeup.

Katherine sneers at the woman. "Do not make me repeat myself."

Scarlet nods and her face morphs from sobs to smiles. Once her makeup is repaired, her assistant wraps a large, white feather boa around her shoulders. She removes her robe, using the boa to cover the more intimate parts of her body, and steps in front of the green screen, as glamorous as always. Words scroll up the teleprompter and she squints, trying to make out her script through the fog of her tears.

"Ladies and gentlemen, do not leave just yet. For we have a surprise in store for you. Three offenders have been very naughty." Scarlet giggles, teasing the audience with her boa. The audience cheers wildly. "You asked for more, so we're giving it to you. In just a few short minutes you'll get a one-of-a-kind fight to the death. Our three bad boys will face off, but only one will survive. Go get refreshed, and we'll be right back with an event you won't want to miss."

"I won't kill them!" Slim shouts. "I won't kill innocent men."

Scarlet's bravado wavers and she rushes back to the arms of her assistant, once again sobbing. Katherine sneers at Slim. "You will have no choice, JP4501. I decide what happens in the Arena. *You* will fight."

The barrel of a gun presses into my spine and I'm forced to take a step forward. I take one long look at Gerard and see the relief letting his features go lax.

He's getting away with murder, again. I can't let this happen. I *won't* let it happen.

-TWENTY-EIGHT-

I SPIN AROUND AND SHOVE THE BARREL OF THE guard's gun up. It fires, and I strike out at the guard with my elbow, just under his helmet. The blow lands on his throat and he stumbles back, dropping his gun. Bear and Slim don't hesitate—they fight back. We all fight back.

Somewhere between the screaming and the firing of guns, Gerard shouts orders into a cell, something about a hovercopter meeting him on the balcony. I break free from the guards and scoop up the abandoned gun. I charge forward and reach out, grabbing Katherine Marsh by the neck, the gun pressed to her temple.

"Tell them to stop! NOW!"

"Back down!" Katherine orders. "Everyone, back down!"

The guards quickly back away. Bear and Slim look around with wild eyes.

"Weapons on the ground! Kick them in front of you!" I press the gun even harder against Katherine's head and she stands firm, not revealing her emotions. The guards drop their weapons and Bear and Slim hurry to pick them up. "Now line up with the technicians against the wall and face it. Do it. Do it!"

They comply and I turn my head to the senators. "Down here, now! Move it, or she gets her head blown off."

"Kill her," Gerard says without emotion. "I won't take orders from an offender."

Bear lifts his gun and fires. It strikes Gerard in the leg and he falls down the steps. Scarlet is once again in a hysterical fit, wailing like a siren. Senator Lindt puts his hands up and moves gracefully down the steps. He turns his large back to face the wall with the others.

"Damn it, can you get her to shut up?" Bear shouts.

"I got it," Slim says. He marches over to Scarlet, who cries even louder as she presses herself against her assistant's chest. Slim grabs her by the arm and pulls her close to him. "I've wanted to do this for as long as I can remember." He presses his lips to her open mouth and the woman falls limp.

The silence is wonderful.

He sets her down, and the technician begins patting her face.

"Don't worry," says Slim. "I have that effect on all women."

"Slim! Get your fat shank over here," Bear orders. "What now, Cal?"

My mind is reeling. For the moment we're in control, but I know it can turn bad at any second. Life in the Arena is anything but predicable. "We'll take Katherine as a hostage. Gerard ordered a hovercopter to pick him up on the balcony. We'll take that."

"Where's the balcony?" Slim asks Gerard. The senator shakes his head and cowers, hands clasped to the wound in his thigh. Slim raises a gun. "I can make you tell me."

"Up there," Katherine says. "Behind the screen. You don't even need a passkey to get out."

"Let's go." I march toward the stairs, Katherine still firmly in my grasp.

Bear steps in front of me, his eyes angrier than I've ever seen. "Wait. We can't leave yet. I've spent the last eleven years in this prison because of this man. It's time he pays for it."

Bear grabs Gerard by the collar of his suit and hauls him toward the green screen. "I'm really going to give the crowd something to cheer for."

"Bear, what are you doing?" Slim asks.

"He has to pay for his crimes!" Bear booms. "He took my life. I'm taking his."

Bear drags a kicking and screaming Gerard across the set, ties him to the bow of the ship, and readies a gun at his head. *Will Bear really kill him like this? Is this what the Arena has done to him—made him a vengeful killer?*

"Calvin, buddy boy, *please* don't do this." The way Gerard looks at me makes me sick, as if we're friends, saying my name while only moments ago he called me a criminal and demanded my death. I hate him. I hate everything about him.

"Don't call me that!" I shout.

"Calvin, I love you."

"You *hate* me! You sent me to this hell."

"Whoa," Slim says, touching my arm. "Let me take her before you accidentally put a bullet in her head." I pass Katherine over to Slim, and he holds his gun against her side. I turn my attention back to Gerard. He's shaking, and I don't blame him. He should be afraid.

"Calvin, please, I knew your mother—"

"Don't you mention my mother. You have no right to even think about her. Had she known what you did to me—to Dad—she would hate you just as much as I do."

"Think about this for a minute," Gerard says, trying to worm his way free. Bear slaps him across the face. "Oh, God, please don't let him kill me this way. Oh, please. Please."

Gerard looks at me pathetically, tears and snot running down his face. Bear laughs. "We're not going to kill you, Senator. You're going to confess your crimes."

Is that what Bear is doing? Yes, a confession! Now is the perfect opportunity to prove my innocence, to gain my freedom from this madness. Gerard has to confess.

Bear forces one of the technicians to power up the cameras. At first the man gives a worried glance to Katherine but she nods her head. The bright lights of the set flick on and Gerard's face fills the monitors in the room.

Gerard shakes his head. "No. I can't. I can't."

Bear crosses back to Gerard and presses his thumb into the bullet wound on Gerard's leg. The senator howls, and Bear gets in his face. "You'll look at the camera and explain that Cal is innocent. You will take full credit for the murder of his father, or I'll give you a matching hole to poke at."

"What I did, I did for Primus," Gerard says through tears. "Please, Calvin. You know history. Think about the American Civil War. Think about Abraham Lincoln. I was only trying to do what he would've done in my position."

"Lincoln wasn't a murderer."

"No, no, but if people stood in his way to unite the Union, he would've done what I did. Your father was against the end of the blue brand. He hated the defectors because they brought disease and poverty to our nation. They brought back sickness like cancer because they were unclean. Oh, God, Calvin. If you'd known what he and the other members of the senate wanted to do, you would've killed him too. You were a sacrifice I had to make to keep going. I'm trying to save Primus. Don't do this. A confession from me will only put people like Lindt and the other senators against the blue brands. I removed your father to save us—to save Mary."

"Shut up! That's not true! You killed him to make yourself Consul. Stop trying to sound so noble."

"Think about it, Calvin. Just think. I'm not Consul—I don't care about being Consul. A war is coming, and we need this country unified, or we'll all be taken out. I did this for Primus—for you!"

"NO! You stole my life from me and threw me into this hell! How is that for *me*?" Before I know it, I pull back on the trigger and the bullet strikes him in the left arm. Gerard screams. Part of me wants to pull the trigger again, only this time catching him in the heart. It would be so easy.

"Are we live?" Bear asks the technician. The man cowers and taps a button on the consul. A red light blinks on the camera and the technician backs away, giving Bear a nod.

"Turn to the camera, Senator," Bear orders. "Tell Primus what you've done."

Gerard trembles like a kicked dog. "Okay … Okay … I killed Thaddeus Sawyer and framed his son for the murder. I drugged Calvin the night before and staged the whole thing. I paid off Judge Isaac to speed up the trial and send Calvin to the Arena. But I did it for the good of the peo—" Bear squeezes down on the wound in his arm and Gerard flinches in pain.

"Keep going," Bear orders.

"I orchestrated the murders of Senators Billings and Watson. I did this thinking I was saving Primus from a much bigger evil. They were trying to unite the senate in something awful. You have to believe me; I did it for Primus—to save thousands of lives. I'm the good guy here."

"Tell them about Doctor Barrett Otis," I shout. "Tell them about how you set him up, too."

"How did you—?" Gerard looks from me to Bear and realization dawns on his face. He hesitates, but nods his head. "Eleven years ago, I falsified information that led to the conviction of Doctor Barrett Otis, who was tried for murder and sentenced to life in the Arena. I also used Judge Isaac to push the trail. I did it because I was heartbroken. The woman I loved had died."

"Liar! You never loved her! Stop lying!"

Bear grabs my arm as I raise my gun once more. "No, Cal. Let it go. He's confessed. It's time to let it go, now."

"The hovercopter's here," Slim says. "Come on, let's go."

I look around the room and see the technicians and guards are turned toward us. The guards have all removed their mirrored helmets, shock and horror prevalent on their very human faces. They now know. We were never criminals. They did all this to innocent men. The only one not looking at us is Senator Lindt. He hasn't taken his angry eyes off Gerard. No doubt his confession is a tragic revelation.

Slim pushes Katherine up the steps leading to the balcony. Bear and I follow.

"Calvin, wait," Gerard calls. "Please, Cal."

I turn back and look him in the eyes, feeling my heart shatter into a million pieces. I wanted Slim and Bear to be wrong about him. I wanted it to be someone else.

"Kill me. Please. Don't let me go into the Arena."

In his eyes I see a glimpse of all the good times we had together—him teaching me how to play chess, what to say to introduce myself to a girl, building the pergola with Mom. In some ways, he was just as much a father as Dad.

I hate him for what he did, but I hate the Arena so much

more. Killing him would be easy—it wouldn't be murder, it would be mercy.

I shake my head. "I was put on this earth to give life, not take it away. I'm sorry, Javier. I'm sorry you didn't learn that lesson early on."

I rush up the steps after Bear while Gerard calls after me.

I push back the screen and head out onto the balcony. The night is cold, but I welcome its freshness. I want to stand there and bask in the wonder of it, but Slim calls for me to hurry.

Bear removes the pilot from the hovercopter and ties him to the balcony's railing. He fits himself in behind the controls and begins pressing buttons. In my wildest dreams, I wouldn't know how to operate a hovercopter, so I'm grateful Bear doesn't seem to be afraid to try anything. I take a seat next to Slim, who still has his gun on Katherine.

"Do we really need her?"

"Have you been pardoned yet?" Slim asks.

I know we should hold her for collateral, but looking at her is only a reminder of all the torture she inflicted. I don't want any reminders. "Let her go."

"Cal, come on, she's our—"

"I said, let her go."

The hovercopter lifts upward and I slide open the door. "Katherine, you'll have to jump. I hope you'll do what's right."

She looks at me with that cold, calculating grin and it makes me want to push her from the craft. "This isn't over,

CS4521. You may be innocent, but you still belong to the Arena."

"I belong to myself. Now, get out."

Katherine jumps, and her fall isn't pretty. I hear her legs crack as she hits the balcony. I try not to feel too bad. A healthy dose of nanorobotics will make her better in no time.

We lift up even higher and Bear shouts for us to close the door. I slide it shut and expect Slim to set into me about how stupid it was for me to let Katherine go, but he doesn't. Instead, he leans back in his seat, closes his eyes, and gives a satisfied sigh of relief. I sit back too, but stare outside the window.

As we fly up over the colosseum, I can't help but marvel at the grandeur of the building, the tall arches, the statues, everything about it making it appear to be exactly what it's not. Behind its illusion of majesty is a world of chaos and death. A world where men become monsters and all meaning and respect for life is nonexistent.

One day, I promise myself, I'll be the one to tear it down. Until then, I'll be free.

To be continued in

THE WALLS OF PRIMUS BOOK TWO

ACKNOWLEDGEMENTS

I am so grateful that I have a wonderful support system of positive individuals who help build me up and remind me to keep going no matter how hard the road becomes. I want to just take a moment to thank them.

First, to Brooklyn, my wife. Thank you for your relentless belief in me. You never let me quit and you always have a reason for me to smile. Thank you for the late nights where I kept you up chatting about a world in which only I could see. It takes a special woman to put up with an absentminded man like me and I'm so happy that you do. To eternity and beyond!

Second, to Ali Cross, my partner in crime. You have been phenomenal in helping me hone this book into what it is now. I couldn't have picked a better friend or critique partner. Thank you for always being there for me and never letting me forget the underlying theme of this book—hope.

My glorious editor, Cas Peace. Thank you for catching all the details that I always seem to gloss over. I feel I'm a better writer because I have you in my corner, couching me on what and what not to do. Xoxo!

Next, I'd like to thank the amazing authors, Jared Garrett, Rebecca Rode, Ilima Todd, Shauna E. Black, and Christine Fonseca for the raving endorsements you gave *Offender.* You boosted my confidence in this project and it's what helped me to keep going.

I'd also like to include the Oquirrh Chapter of the League of Utah Writers. You guys all rock and have always been a huge support to my writing journey.

To my sister, Stephanie, for always being my cheerleader.

To Jennifer A. Nielsen and J. Scott Savage, two amazing authors and friends who never let me give up.

To my wonderful readers, who give me a reason to keep doing what I doing.

And lastly, to my Heavenly Father, who has blessed me with more miracles than I deserve.

THANK YOU, ALL!

ABOUT THE AUTHOR

Since a young age Michael Brooks has been told he was best at making things up. If it wasn't concocting a lie to get out of trouble, it was creating wild tales about aliens abducting cows from the barn, or stories of ghosts haunting the woods that surrounded their farmhouse in Missouri. Now he's all grown up, earned a degree in creative writing, and has turned his passion for "making things up" into a profession..

He lives in Utah with his beautiful wife, their five amazing kiddos, four crazy chicken, too many fish to count, an impressive wand collection, and one or two invisible dragons. He also writes and illustrates stories for younger readers under the name Mikey Brooks. You can find more about him and his other books at www.mikeybrooks.com.

Keep in touch and join Michael's Newsletter:
http://eepurl.com/gmXjMT

Follow Mikey on Social Media:

Facebook: facebook.com/writtenbymikey
Twitter: twitter.com/mikeybr00ks
Instagram: instagram.com/insidemikeysworld

If you enjoyed this books please consider leaving a review.

www.ingramcontent.com/pod-product-compliance
Lightning Source LLC
Chambersburg PA
CBHW020256030826
48979CB00026B/1271/J

* 9 7 8 1 9 3 9 9 9 3 8 4 7 *